시조,
서정시로 새기다

Encounters with the Korean Lyrical Spirit
An Anthology of Sijo

맹사성, 이현보, 이황, 정철, 신흠, 윤선도, 신계영, 이휘일, 황진이, 김천택, 박효관 지음

고정희, 저스틴 M. 바이런-데이비스 편역

Written by

Maeng Sa-seong, Lee Hyun-bo, Lee Hwang, Jeong Cheol, Shin Heum, Yun Seon-do,

Shin Gye-young, Lee Hwi-il, Hwang Jin-i, Kim Cheon-taek, Park Hyo-gwan

Selected and translated by

Ko Jeong-hee and Justin M. Byron-Davies

시조,
서정시로 새기다

Encounters with the Korean Lyrical Spirit
An Anthology of Sijo

차례

Contents

서문
Preface

시조는 3행으로 이루어진 한국어 시가로, 14세기부터 19세기까지 약 오백여 년 동안 노래로 불리었다. 이 시기 시조는 한국인들의 슬픔, 기쁨, 좌절 등 다양한 감정을 표현하는 주요한 서정적 도구였다. 현대 독자들은 시조를 감상하며 한국인의 서정적 심성을 느낄 수 있을 뿐만 아니라, 조선시대 학자이자 관료였던 '사대부'들의 정제된 중세 철학도 이해할 수 있다.

이 책은 한국의 언어와 문화를 공부하는 외국인 학생들과, 한국 문화에 관심이 있는 국내외 독자들에게 시조를 소개하기 위해 영문으로 번역한 작업물이다. 이

Sijo is a three-line verse form which was written in the Korean vernacular and sung by Koreans for over five hundred years from the fourteenth to the nineteenth century. During this time, sijo was the major lyrical tool for Koreans to express emotions such as sorrow, delight, and frustration. By reading sijo, modern readers are able to feel the lyrical spirit of the Korean people and understand the medieval philosophy which was refined by upper-class scholar-officials known as 'Sadaebu (Neo-Confucian literati)'.

책의 가치는 다른 영역(英譯) 시조 선집들과는 달리, 시조를 전공한 한국 학자(고정희)와 영국 중세 문학을 전공한 영국 학자(저스틴 M. 바이런-데이비스)가 공동으로 작업한 결과라는 데 있다. 시조를 영어로 번역하는 과정에서, 고정희는 가능한 한 원문의 의미를 그대로 옮기고자 한 반면 저스틴 M. 바이런-데이비스는 시의 운율과 영문의 미묘한 차이에 대한 민감한 감수성을 바탕으로 원문의 뉘앙스를 영문에서도 전달하는 데 초점을 두었다. 서로 강조하는 지점이 다르다 보니 역자들은 2년 반이 넘는 기간 동안 번역 작업에 몰두할 수밖에 없었다. 처음에는 두 역자가 서울에서 만나 의견을 나누었고 이후에는 스카이프를 통해 인터넷으로 소통하며 작업을 하였다.

시조와 영국 중세 문학이라는 상호보완적인 전문성을 지닌 역자들의 공동 작업은 서로에게도 새로운 것을 배워나가는 과정이었다. 시조의 서정적 특질을 전달하기 위해 역자들은 시조의 한 행 한 행을 번역할 때마다 무수히 많은 토론을 거쳤다. 번역 작업 초기에 두 역자는 단순한 직역으로는 시조의 본질적인 의미와 뉘앙스를 전달할 수 없다는 사실을 깨달았다. 이에 시조 시행

Our goal in making this translation is to introduce sijo to students of the Korean language and literature as well as to those with a general interest in Korean culture. Our book differs from other anthologies of sijo in English translation in being the result of collaboration between a Korean academic who specialises in sijo and a British academic who specialises in medieval English literature. Justin's expertise in medieval English literature, including poetry, means that he is attuned to the cadences of verse and sensitive to the subtleties of language. His dedication and persistence in seeking to convey the nuances of the original Korean in English translation complemented Jeong-hee's breadth of knowledge of this genre and her preference for adhering to the original meaning wherever possible. This is why our work has taken two and a half years to complete – initially in Seoul and later in cyberspace through the indispensable medium of Skype.

This pooling of complementary expertise evolved

에 대한 각자의 이해를 명확히 확인하고 서로의 통찰을 교환하면서 조금씩 진전된 번역을 얻을 수 있었다. 이 과정을 더욱 괴롭게 만들었던 것은 번역이라는 작업 자체에 내재한 딜레마였다. 시조 전문가인 역자는 기본적으로 번역 결과가 원문의 의미에서 벗어나지 않게끔 노력하였으나, 두 언어 사이의 차이와 문화적인 특수성으로 인해 특정 부분들은 직접적인 번역이 거의 불가능하였다. 역자 간 소통을 통해 축어적인 번역보다 '대안적 번역'을 찾는 방향으로 타협이 이루어졌다. '대안적 번역'이란 원문과 번역문이 일대일로 엄격하게 대응하지는 않더라도, 더 정확하게 원문의 의미와 뉘앙스를 전달하는 번역을 의미한다. 영국인 역자가 이 과정에서 중요한 역할을 담당하였다.

이 책의 번역을 평가하는 일은 독자들에게 달려 있다. 그러나 다른 나라의 독자들도 시조에 쉽게 접근하고 시조를 아름다운 서정시로서 감상할 수 있게 만들고자 한 이 책의 목표를 어느 정도는 달성하였다고 생각한다. 이 선집에는 11명의 뛰어난 시인들이 지은 중요한 시조들이 소개되어 있다. 독자들이 각자의 나라와 문학 장르, 시대를 넘어 시조의 시적 자질과 서정적 형식을 두

into a learning process for us both. In order to deliver the 'spirit' of sijo, we had to meet countless times to discuss each poem, line by line. From the outset we realised that a direct translation would be inadequate to convey the essential meaning and nuances of these sijo. Therefore, these sessions involved exchanging insights, clarifying each other's understanding of specific lines which, prior to this, occasionally diverged, and even negotiation. This was a somewhat arduous journey because of a particular dilemma. As a specialist in sijo, Jeong-hee naturally sought to adhere to the original meaning. However, she lamented the impossibility of translating certain segments directly, whether due to differences between the two languages, or culturally specific references. As the prospect of achieving the desired more direct translation receded, the value of our discussions became increasingly apparent. The necessary compromises involved deviating from a verbatim translation and instead searching for an alternative, less rigid but

루 경험할 수 있기를 희망한다.

　마지막으로 이 책의 출판을 맡아 준 아시아 출판사에 심심한 감사를 표한다. 특별한 사랑과 인내심, 열정과 관심으로 우리의 작업을 지지해 준 각자의 가족에게도 깊은 감사의 마음을 전하고 싶다. 한국인 역자 고정희는 2015년에서 2016년까지 영국 서리대학교 '영어와 언어' 학과에서 연구년을 보냈다. 그때 영국인 역자 저스틴 M. 바이런-데이비스는 같은 학과에서 박사학위 과정을 이미 수료한 상황이어서 당시에는 서로 알지 못했다. 두 역자들을 온라인상으로 소개하여 2016년 서울에서 첫 만남을 가질 수 있도록 주선한 다이안 워트 교수께 감사 드린다. 또한 한국인 역자를 영국 서리대학의 방문학자로 초빙하고, 따뜻한 지원을 아끼지 않았던 사라 미셸로티 선생님께도 특별한 감사를 드린다. 무엇보다도, 지구 반대편에 있었던 두 학자의 만남을 이끌어주신 하나님께 감사 드린다.

　2019년 4월
　고정희와 저스틴 M. 바이런-데이비스가 함께 씀.

ultimately more precise translation. Justin played an instrumental role in this endeavour.

Our readers will judge for themselves, but we feel that we have attained our goal of translating sijo that can be appreciated as beautiful lyrical poetry and making it accessible to a wide international readership. In this anthology we introduce some of the most influential sijo of eleven renowned Korean poets. We hope our readers will be able to appreciate the poetic features of sijo and broaden their exposure to this lyrical form, encompassing a different country, genre and era.

We would like to express our appreciation to ASIA Publishers for publishing our book. We would like to thank our respective families who supported this work, whether by their love, patience, tolerance, enthusiasm, or general interest. We are fortunate to have them as part of our life. Our paths did not cross during Jeong-hee's time as visiting scholar in the School of English and Languages in the University of Surrey in the United Kingdom from 2015–2016 because Justin had completed his doctoral research in the department by then. Therefore, we owe a special debt of gratitude to Professor Diane Watt for introducing us online, thereby enabling our first meeting in Seoul in 2016. Jeong-hee would also like to express her appreciation to the former Deputy Head of School Sarah Michelotti who invited her to the Department and provided her with warm-hearted support during her time in Surrey. Most importantly, we thank God for allowing two academics from the opposite sides of the globe to encounter each other.

April 2019

Ko Jeong-hee and Justin M. Byron-Davies

도입
Introduction

시조는 음수율을 가진 3개의 시행으로 이루어진 운문이다.[1] 하나의 시행은 보통 14개에서 16개의 음절로 이루어져 있으며, 각 음절들은 4개의 음보로 나뉜다. 시조율격의 유일한 원칙은, 시조가 음수율을 가지고 있어 각 음보마다 배분되는 음절의 수가 정해져 있다는 것이다. 아래의 시조에서 볼 수 있듯이, 이상적인 시조 율격은 첫 번째 행과 두 번째 행의 음절수가 3-4-3-4의 패턴을

---

1 시조의 율격을 음수율로 볼 것인가, 음보율로 볼 것인가는 연구사에서 오랜 쟁점이 되어 왔는데, 여기서는 고정희, '고전시가 율격의 교육 내용 연구'(《국어교육연구》 29집, 서울대 국어교육연구소, 2012)에 의거하여 음수율로 설명한다.

Sijo is three-line verse which has syllabic metre. Each line has only fourteen to sixteen syllables which are distributed in four feet. Since the prosody of sijo is syllabic, the only recognised metrical principle is the number of syllables per foot. The ideal metre of sijo is a first and second line with a 3-4-3-4 pattern, and a last line with a 3-5 (6/7)-4-3 pattern, as seen below.

보이고, 마지막 행은 3-5 (6/7)-4-3의 패턴을 보인다.

유란幽蘭이(3) 재곡在谷하니(4) 자연自然이(3) 듯디 죠희(4)

백운白雲이(3) 재산在山하니(4) 자연自然이(3) 보디 죠해(4)

이 중에(3) 피미일인彼美一人을(5) 더옥 닛디(4) 못하얘(3)

첫 번째 행과 두 번째 행에서 같은 패턴이 반복되면, 독자들은 음수율이 계속 유지될 것이라는 기대를 하기 마련이다. 그러나 마지막 행에서 급변하는 음수율은 독자의 기대를 뒤집는다. 시조에는 마지막 행의 첫 번째 음보가 반드시 세 개의 음절이 되어야 한다는 비교적 엄격한 규칙이 있으며, 두 번째 음보에서 비상하게 긴 음절수를 보였다가 세 번째와 네 번째 음보에서는 음절수가 서서히 줄어든다. 두 번째 음보에서 긴장감이 조성되었다가 이어지는 음보들에서 이완되는 율격적 변화를 통해 단순한 형식인 시조가 시인들의 생각과 감정을 역동적으로 구현할 수 있었다. 또한 시조 각 시행의 중간에는 짧은 휴지(caesura)가 있어 시행을 의미론적으로 이분한다. 이분된 반행끼리는 서로 대칭을 이루는 구조를 형성하며, 각 행의 마지막에는 보다 긴 휴지가 있다.

유란幽蘭이(3) 재곡在谷하니(4) 자연自然이(3) 듯디 죠희(4)

백운白雲이(3) 재산在山하니(4) 자연自然이(3) 보디 죠해(4)

이 중에(3) 피미일인彼美一人을(5) 더옥 닛디(4) 못하얘(3)

The repeating pattern of the first and second line causes the reader to expect that this metre will be sustained. However, the reader's anticipation is always betrayed by the sudden modification of the last line's syllabic metre. It was a rigid regulation that the first foot of the last line had to be composed of three syllables. Then there follow unusually long syllables in the second foot which gradually reduce in number in the third and fourth feet. This modification serves to create tension and subsequent relief, both formally and semantically. Even though sijo is notable for the brevity of its form, poets can express their thoughts and feelings dynamically. Also, there is a short caesura in the middle of each line, which creates semantic division and symmetry. There is also a long caesura at the end of each line.

Unfortunately, we cannot retain this metrical feature in translation. The best we can do is to deliver the spirit of sijo, which is far from a straightforward task. Despite

그러나 시조의 율격은 영문 번역 과정에서 그대로 유지하기 힘든 자질이다. 대신 역자들은 시조의 서정적 특질을 충실히 전달하고자 애썼다. 비록 번역을 통해 율격적인 자질을 그대로 구현할 수 없더라도, 영역(英譯) 시조는 그 나름대로의 가치를 지닌다. 시조는 특유의 시적 이미지들을 통해 새로운 존재론적 시각들을 제공하기 때문이다. 이하에서는 시조의 역사를 간략하게 서술하여 시조에 나타나 있는 특유의 시적 이미지들을 독자들이 이해할 수 있게 돕고자 한다.

시조의 역사는 역성혁명을 통해 고려 왕조(918-1392)를 멸망시키고 조선 왕조(1392-1897)를 창업하는 데 동참했던 사대부들의 출현과 함께 시작된다. 사대부들은 조선이라는 새로운 나라에서 자신들의 이상적인 정치를 실현하기 위해 노력하였다. 이들은 한문학에 전문적 소양을 갖추고 조정에서 임금을 보좌하며 19세기까지 조선의 지배 세력으로 군림하였는데, 이들이 자신들의 철학과 감정을 표현하고자 향유하였던 문학이 시조이다.

이 선집의 제1부에는 사대부들이 쓴 고전 시조들이 실려 있다. 이 시조들은 한국인들조차도 지루하고, 지

the loss of the metrical feature, sijo in translation still has intrinsic value for readers all over the world. Sijo contains unique poetic images that offer fresh ontological perspectives. A brief history of the genre will help the reader's understanding.

Sijo appeared in Korean literary history with the emergence of the Neo-Confucian literati of the Joseon dynasty (1392-1897), which was established by revolution and replaced the Goryeo dynasty (918-1392). These founders of the new dynasty tried to realise the ideal regime in the country by supporting the king. Until the nineteenth century, Neo-Confucian literati dominated politics, serving in the royal court and sharing their expertise in Chinese literature. They entertained themselves with sijo to express their philosophy and emotions.

Part one of this anthology contains classical sijo written by these Neo-Confucian literati. Even Koreans have the misconception that their sijo is boring, overly rigid, and lacking in lyrical emotions. However, the poets never impose their philosophy on their audience. Instead, they express their impressions about the harmony of nature, such as in the four seasons cycle,

나치게 엄숙하며 서정적인 감정이 결여되어 있다고 오해하는 작품들이다. 하지만 시인들은 결코 시조를 통해 자신들의 철학을 강요하지 않았다. 그보다는 사계절의 순환과 같은 자연의 조화에 대한 감동을 노래하였고, 모든 존재자들을 그들에게 마땅한 자리에 존재하게끔 만드는 임금의 은혜에 대한 감사를 표현하였다. 다음의 시조에 그러한 감동이 잘 나타나 있다.

유란幽蘭이 재곡在谷하니 자연自然이 듯디 죠희

백운白雲이 재산在山하니 자연自然이 보디 죠해

이 중에 피미일인彼美一人을 더옥 닛디 못하얘

이 작품은 이황(1501-1570)이 창작한 시조이다. 이황은 당대에는 물론 오늘날까지도 가장 위대한 성리학자로 여겨지는 인물이다. 보다시피 그의 시조에는 幽蘭(유란), 在谷(재곡), 自然(자연), 白雲(백운), 在山(재산), 彼美一人(피미일인)처럼 수많은 한자어들이 들어 있는데, 이러한 단어들은 독자들로 하여금 그의 철학에 입문할 수 있도록 이끌어 준다. 이황은 성리학자로서 자연에 존재하는 모든 사물들이 자연의 섭리를 보여 주는

and appreciation for the king's benevolence, which in theory holds all elements of existence in their correct place. This may be illustrated by looking at the following sijo as an example.

Shaded orchids in the valley,
Natural virtue of their subtle scent.
White clouds caress the mountainsides,
A joyful balm to the sight.
In the midst of these things,
One more beautiful reigns in my heart!

This sijo was written by Lee Hwang (1501-1570) who was regarded as a great Neo-Confucian scholar in his time, a reputation that has endured to the present day. As the reader will note, his sijo contains numerous Chinese characters such as 幽蘭 (유란 / shaded orchids), 在谷 (재곡 / in the valley), 自然 (자연 / natural virtue), 白雲 (백운 / white clouds), 在山 (재산 / caress the mountainsides), and 彼美一人 (피미일인 / one more beautiful). These key terms provide apertures into his philosophy. As a Neo-Confucian scholar, he believed that every common thing in

가시적인 예시가 된다고 여겼다. 이 평범한 사물들은 선정을 베푸는 임금의 은혜 아래서 하늘이 그들에게 본질적으로 부여한 존재의 이유를 실현하고 있다.

이황의 철학에 대한 선지식이 없는 독자들도 이 책을 통해 그가 사소한 자연물들까지 친밀하게 여겼다는 점을 느낄 수 있다. 이황은 자연물들이 인간의 관심이나 주목과는 상관없이 자신들의 존재이유를 스스로 구현하고 있다는 점에 감탄한다. 예를 들어, 시의 화자는 '골짜기에 있는 난초'가 비록 인간의 눈에는 보이지 않더라도 '은은한 향기'를 가지고 있기 때문에 '자연히 향기 맡기 좋아'라고 말한다. '산을 감싸 도는 흰구름'은 영원히 존재하는 두 가지 자연물이 서로에게 조화로운 동반자가 되는 것을 의미한다. 이 광경은 화자의 마음을 기쁨으로 채워 주어, '자연히 보기 좋아'라고 감탄하게 만든다. '이 중에'는 화자 자신이 조화와 질서의 일부가 됨을 느끼는 순간을 표현한다. 하늘은 임금의 통치가 얼마나 은혜로운가에 따라 자신의 섭리를 조화롭게 펼치기 때문에, 조화와 질서는 임금이 은혜로운 통치를 하고 있음을 의미하기도 한다. 화자는 자연물들의 모습에 감격하여 '저 한 미인을 더욱 닛디 못하얘'라고 외치

nature is a tangible example of providence, with its reason for existence endowed naturally by heaven, under the king's benevolence.

Even those readers without any prior knowledge of Lee Hwang's philosophy will gain from this translation a sense of his affinity with the small natural things which have a reason for existence that is independent of human concerns and priorities. For example, 'Shaded orchids in the valley' have the 'natural virtue of their subtle scent' even though they are invisible to human sight. 'White clouds caress the mountainsides' means two ever-present sights in nature which form a harmonious company, a sight that fills the speaker's mind with delight. In the line 'In the midst of these things', the speaker feels like he is part of this harmony and order and he knows this is the case only when the king reigns benevolently because heaven extends this harmony according to the degree of the king's benevolence. Elated, the speaker cries 'one more beautiful reigns in my heart!' Here, 'one more beautiful' indicates the king.

It is not my intention to persuade readers to empathise with the speaker's elation over the king's

는데, '저 한 미인'이란 바로 임금을 가리킨다.

역자가 여기에서 임금의 은혜에 대한 시적 화자의 감격에 공감하라고 독자들을 설득하려는 것은 아니다. 그보다 다음과 같은 장면을 상상해 보도록 권유하고 싶다. 고요하고 깊은 골짜기를 산책하다가 사람의 눈길을 피해 혼자 은은한 향기를 발하고 있는 난초를 우연히 발견한다. 누가 바라봐 주지 않아도 자신의 존재이유를 스스로 구현하고 있는 난초의 향기는 사람으로 하여금 흰 구름을 비롯한 주변을 돌아보게 하며, 그러한 자연물들이 왜 존재하는가를 생각하게 한다. '그들이 왜 존재하는가'라는 질문은, 극도로 경쟁적인 현대사회에서 존재이유를 생각할 겨를 없이 하루하루를 살아가는 우리들에게도 더할 나위 없이 중요하다. 역자들은 독자들이 시조의 세계 속에서 자신만의 은신처를 발견할 수 있기를 바란다.

이 책에서는 시조가 각 시행의 가운데에 휴지를 두어 시행을 의미론적으로 이분한다는 사실을 근거로 원문의 한 행을 두 행으로 나누었다. 이러한 시행의 분할은 독자들로 하여금 시조를 산문보다는 운문으로서 감상하게 하고, 작품 세계를 더욱 수월하게 경험하도록 도와줄 것

benevolence. I would rather recommend imagining the scene where you are strolling in a deep valley in tranquillity and happen to find a shaded orchid hiding itself from human attention while it realises its raison d'être by emitting its subtle scent. This scent prompts a person to consider their entire surroundings, including the white cloud, and ask why they exist. This question is still relevant to modern human beings, especially in our extremely competitive societies, in which there is a real danger of losing a sense of the reason for existence day by day. It is the translators' hope that the reader will find a secret shelter in this world of sijo which is presented to them here.

We divided each line into two based on the fact that sijo has a caesura in the middle of each line which divides the line into two parts semantically. This division will facilitate the reading experience, allowing sijo to be read as poetry rather than prose. As academics who have studied and taught poetry, we are conscious of how readers will read sijo as poetry in English translation. Our most important decision was which sijo to include.

Here I feel a confession is in order. I selected the

이다. 역자들은 시를 공부하고 가르쳐 온 학자들로서 어떻게 해야 독자들이 영문으로 번역된 시조를 시로서 감상할 수 있을지를 고심하였고, 또한 어떤 시조를 선집에 포함시킬지를 결정하는 데에도 심혈을 기울였다.

고백하건대 역자는 스스로가 가장 좋아하는 시조들을 선별하였다. 역자는 오랜 시간 한국 고전시가의 서정적 특질을 공부하면서 어째서 특정 시조가 나에게 더 영감을 주는지를 물어 왔고, 스스로의 존재론적 관심을 되돌아보게 하는 시조들에 매력을 느낀다는 사실을 발견하였다. 따라서 엄밀히 말해 이 선집은 편파적이고 주관적일 수도 있다. 그러나 역자가 스스로 감동을 받지 못한다면 어떻게 독자들로 하여금 감동을 느끼도록 만들 수 있겠는가? 이러한 기준으로, 제1부에서는 수많은 사대부들의 시조 가운데서도 〈강호사시가〉, 〈어부단가〉, 정철 시조, 신흠 시조와 함께 〈도산십이곡〉을 선별하였다.

제1부의 시조들 중에서 신흠(1566-1628)의 시조는 이황이 남긴 유산과는 대비되는 특징을 보인다는 점에서 주목할 만하다. 신흠은 다른 시조 시인들처럼 조정의 관료였다. 그러나 조정에서 쫓겨나는 비극적인 개인

sijo that I love most. I have studied the lyrical feature of medieval Korean poetry for a long time because I am attracted to lyrical poetry that prompts me to consider ontological concerns and why a particular sijo inspires me. By definition, this anthology is partial and subjective. However, how could one enable the reader to be moved without being personally impacted by the sijo in question? Because of this partiality, in part one I selected *Twelve songs at Dosan* along with *Song of the four seasons at the lake world* and *Short songs of a fisherman*, as well as sijo by Jeong-Cheol and Shin Heum, from an abundance of sijo written by Neo-Confucian literati.

The sijo of Shin Heum (1566-1628) provides a notable counterpoint to Lee Hwang's legacy in part one. Shin Heum was a court bureaucrat like other sijo poets of the past. However, his tragic personal experience of being banished from the court compelled him to view nature from different perspectives with his characteristic scepticism regarding the providence of heaven. The title 'Songs by an exiled old man' conveys a sense of tragedy and melancholy even before the reader approaches his sijo.

사로 말미암아 하늘의 섭리를 회의하게 되었고, 자연을 다른 시각으로 바라보게 되었다. '쫓겨난 노인의 노래(방옹시여)'라는 제목을 보면, 그의 시조를 읽기 전부터 비극적이고 우울한 느낌을 받게 된다.

제2부에는 시조 장르의 정점에 올라 있는 윤선도(1587-1671)의 〈어부사시사〉를 실었다. 윤선도의 작품을 생략 없이 모두 싣기로 한 것은 매우 어려운 결정이었다. 이 작품은 총 40수나 되어 다른 시조와 비교할 때 양적인 불균형이 생겨나기 때문이다. 그러나 불균형을 낳게 된다 하더라도, 다음과 같은 이유들로 전문을 수록하는 것이 불가피하다고 판단하였다. 첫째, 윤선도는 한국 문학사에서 가장 뛰어난 시조 시인이다. 둘째는 더욱 중요한 이유로서, 그의 시조 40수를 읽어 나가다 보면 다른 시조에서 만났던 대부분의 이미지들과 다시 조우할 수 있으며, 시조 장르 자체에 대한 이해를 더욱 풍요롭게 할 수 있기 때문이다.

제3부는 사대부들의 전원 시조를 소개한다. 17세기에 이르면, 시조 시인들이 성리학의 철학적 사고보다 그들의 실제 생활을 시조에 반영하는 경향들이 나타난다. 신계영(1577-1669)은 조정의 관료였지만 말년에

Part two focuses on the zenith of the sijo genre with the sijo of Yun Seon-do (1587-1671). It was a difficult decision to translate Yun Seon-do's *Song of a fisherman's four seasons* without omission. It is composed of forty stanzas which creates an imbalance in terms of quantity compared to other poets' sijo. This imbalance was unavoidable, however, due to the following reasons. The first is that Yun Seon-do is the most renowned sijo poet in Korean history. The second more crucial reason is that as the reader progresses through his forty stanzas, they will re-encounter most of the images that they met in the other poets' sijo and obtain a better understanding of the genre itself.

Part three introduces pastoral sijo written by members of the Neo-Confucian literati. During the seventeenth century, sijo poets tended to reflect their real life in their sijo rather than Neo-Confucian philosophical thought. Shin Gye-young (1577-1669) was a poet and court bureaucrat. In his later career, he lived in his local province (Chungcheong province) and this rural life is reflected in his sijo. Lee Hwi-il (1619-1672) was a member of the literati in Gyeongsang province who did not serve at the court. Those poets

는 충청도 지방에 거처하며 시골에서의 삶의 모습을 시조에 반영하였다. 이휘일(1619-1672)은 경상도 지역의 문인으로서 조정에서 관료 생활을 하지는 않았다. 신계영, 이휘일과 같이 고향에 머무는 것을 선호했던 시인들은 사대부들이 이상으로 생각했던 자연의 섭리 대신, 일상적인 삶의 관찰과 전원적인 분위기를 시조에 담았다.

제4부는 사대부가 아닌 다른 계층의 시인들이 쓴 시조들로 구성되어 있다. 기생은 양반 계층 남성들의 연회의 동반자로서 음악과 시로 유흥을 제공했던 여성들이다. 기생은 15세기부터 시조 역사에 등장하여 사적 주제인 사랑과 이별을 노래함으로써 전통적 정전을 바꾸어 놓았다. 기생들은 사랑하는 님과 헤어졌을 때의 슬픔을 노래한다. 사실 사랑하는 님에게 버려진 여인의 슬픔은 남성 작가들이 임금에 대한 절대적인 충성심을 전달하는 관습적인 은유로 활용해 오던 것이다. (이 선집은 사랑을 주제로 한 시조들을 따로 선별하지는 않았으나, 이러한 경향은 정철과 신흠의 시조에서 엿볼 수 있다.) 그러나 황진이(16세기)의 시조는 자신의 실제 연인에 대해 비판적이며, 심지어는 연인을 자신보다 열등

who preferred to stay in their home town observed everyday life and evoked the pastoral atmosphere instead of focusing on the Neo-Confucian idea of the nature of providence.

Part four consists of sijo written by other classes in society. Kisaeng were women who provided company and entertainment (music and poetry) for upper-class men. They emerged in the history of sijo from the fifteenth century. Kisaeng changed the tradition of the canon while writing on personal themes of love and loss. When their lovers departed, the Kisaeng would sing a lament. Male writers used this lament of the abandoned woman in their own sijo as a conventional metaphor that conveyed their absolute loyalty to the king. (Although these love-themed sijo do not appear in this anthology, there are glimpses of their type in the sijo of Jeong Cheol and Shin Heum.) The sijo of Hwang Jin-i (16c) is critical of these lovers, even viewing them as inferior and unworthy of their respect, and expresses feelings of indifference towards her lovers' passion.

From the eighteenth century, another stream emerged from the middle-class men who contributed to the sijo

하거나 존중 받을 가치가 없는 사람으로 간주하는 경향을 보인다. 나아가, 연인들의 관심에 무심한 반응을 보이는 등 남성 작가들의 사랑 노래와 확연히 구분되는 특징을 지닌다.

18세기부터는 중인 계층 남성에 의한 시조 장르의 새로운 흐름이 나타났다. 중인 계층 남성들은 시조 장르에 기여하며 이후 시조의 가창문화를 이끄는 핵심인물들이 된다. 이들의 시조가 사대부들의 시조와 어떻게 다른지를 보이기 위해 이 책에서는 김천택(18세기)의 시조와 박효관(19세기)의 시조를 수록하였다.

앞서 언급한 내용들을 통해 역자가 시조를 소개하는 까닭이 여러 나라의 독자들과 시조의 서정적 이미지를 함께 나누고 싶기 때문이라는 점을 알 수 있을 것이다. 역자들은 시조를 감상하는 경험이 서정시에 대한 독자들의 감수성을 넓히는 기회를 줄 수 있을 것으로 믿고, 시조가 독자들에게 한 편의 서정시처럼 감상 될 수 있도록 번역하는 데 최선을 다하였다.

이 책에는 시조의 원문과 영문 번역이 나란히 제시되어 있다. 중세국어로 쓰여 있는 시조에 현대 독자들이 쉽게 접근할 수 있도록, 중세국어에서만 쓰였던 철자를

genre and subsequently became dominant figures who led the culture of sung sijo. I selected sijo written by Kim Cheon-taek (18c) and sijo written by Park Hyo-gwan (19c) to show how their sijo are different from the poetry of the Neo-Confucian literati.

The reader will infer from what I have mentioned above that my intention in introducing sijo is to share its lyrical images with an international audience. I believe that reading sijo gives readers the opportunity to broaden their sensibility toward lyrical poetry. For this reason, we have endeavoured to make our translation read like lyrical poetry.

The original sijo have been printed along with the translation with slight modifications. Because the sijo were written in medieval Korean, we judged it necessary to modernise the spelling in order to achieve our stated goal of creating an accessible translation for modern readers. Additionally, we have provided some notes to assist the reader's understanding of the more obscure and unfamiliar items of vocabulary and expressions. We have confined these notes to where we think they are necessary and sought to make them as concise as possible so as not to divert the reader's

현대화할 필요가 있었다. 다만 원문을 고치는 것은 가급적 최소한으로 제한하였다. 영문 번역에서는 모호하거나 낯선 어휘와 표현에 대한 이해를 돕기 위해 주석을 제공하였다. 주석은 꼭 필요하다고 생각한 부분에서만 최대한 간략하게 제공하였는데, 주석이 시조 자체에 대한 주의를 흩뜨리지 않도록 하기 위해서이다. 우리는 독자들이 자신의 직관을 바탕으로 주어진 정보로부터 시조의 의미를 추론할 수 있다고 믿는다. 아무쪼록 이 선집의 독자들이 시조의 세계를 엿보고, 그 안에서 한동안 거닐며 의미 있는 통찰과 위로를 얻을 수 있기를 기대한다.

고정희 씀.

attention from the sijo itself. We believe that the reader's instinct will enable them to make their own inferences from the given information. It is our hope that readers of this anthology will be able to glimpse the beautiful world of sijo and walk around in it for a while, perhaps gaining insights and finding solace there.

Ko Jeong-hee

1부
Part 1

사대부들의 고전적인 시조

Classical sijo of Neo-Confucian literati

강호사시가 江湖四時歌

강호江湖에 봄이 드니 미친 흥興이 절로 난다

탁료濁醪 계변溪邊에 금린어錦鱗魚 안주로다

이 몸이 한가閑暇해옴도 역군은亦君恩 이샷다

강호江湖에 녀름이 드니 초당草堂에 일이 업다

유신有信한 강파江波는 보내느니 바람이로다

이 몸이 서늘해옴도 역군은亦君恩 이샷다

강호江湖에 가을이 드니 고기마다 살져 잇다

소정小艇에 그믈 시러 흘리 띄여 더뎌 두고

이 몸이 소일消日해옴도 역군은亦君恩 이샷다

Song of the four seasons
at the lake world

Maeng Sa-seong

As spring arrives to the rivers and lakes,
Elation rises within myself.
At the side of the brook with makkoli,[1]
Savouring side dishes of fresh fish.
Tranquil life bestowed upon me
By the king's benevolence.

As summer arrives at the rivers and lakes,
I am free from labour at the thatched cabin.
Faithful river's flow
Imparts fresh breeze.
Cooling caress
Of the king's benevolence.

As Autumn arrives at the lake,
The fish are fattening.
From the small boat I cast the net upon the water,
Letting it float.
Until the day is extinguished,
I bask in the king's benevolence.

강호江湖에 겨월이 드니 눈 기픠 자히 남다

삿갓 빗기 쓰고 누역縷繹으로 오슬 삼아

이 몸이 칩지 아니해옴도 역군은亦君恩 이샷다

『청구영언』

Winter has arrived at the lake,
A blanket of snow deeper than a foot.
I am dressed in a straw raincoat and a wide-
    brimmed hat,
Tilted nonchalantly.
The wonder of his majesty's benevolence,
Sheltering me in this winter chill.

어부단가 漁父短歌

이현보 李賢輔

이 중에 시름 업스니 어부漁父의 생애生涯로다

일엽一葉 편주扁舟를 만경파萬頃波에 띄여 두고

인세人世를 다 니젯거니 날 가는 줄을 안가

구버는 천심녹수千尋綠水 도라보니 만첩청산萬疊靑山

십장十丈 홍진紅塵이 언매나 가련는고

강호江湖에 월백月白하거든 더옥 무심無心 하얘라

청하靑荷에 밥을 싸고 녹류綠柳에 고기 께여

노적蘆荻 화총花叢에 배 매야 두고

일반一般 청의미淸意味를 어늬 분分이 아르실고

Short songs of a fisherman

Lee Hyun-bo

In the meantime,
The life of the fisherman displaces all cares.
I let the small boat float
On ten thousand furrows of waves.
I forget the world completely,
Unaware of the passing days.

Peering at bottomless depths of green;
Behind, the limitless blue mountain peaks.
Beyond the reach of the red dust
Which obscures the outside world.
As the white moon reflects upon the surface,
I grow indifferent to that world.

Wrapping rice in a green lotus leaf,
Fishes pierced on a willow branch.
At the place of the reeds and flowering shrubs
I moor my boat.
Who but the discerning
Knows this refreshing taste?

산두山頭에 한운閑雲이 기起하고 수중水中에 백구비

　白鷗飛라

무심無心코 다정多情하 니 이 두 거시로다

일생一生애 시름을 닛고 너를 조차 노로리라

장안長安을 도라보니 북궐北闕이 천리千里로다

어주漁舟에 누어신들 니즌 스치 이시랴

두어라 내 시름 아니라 제세현濟世賢이 업스랴

『청구영언』

An indolent cloud caresses the mountain head,
Above the river a white seagull[2] glides.
Indifference and empathy of both
Towards me.
Freed as all cares recede,
I reach for a life in harmony with you.

Recalling life back in the capital;
How far away the north palace seems!
Even as I recline in my fishing boat,
I cannot forget my king.
Let the past recede! Anxiety need no longer
   oppress.
I await the sage who will save the world.

도산십이곡 陶山十二曲

이황 李滉

도산육곡지일 陶山六曲之一

기일其一

이런들 엇더하며 져런들 엇더하료

초야草野 우생愚生이 이러타 엇더하료

하믈며 천석고황泉石膏肓을 고쳐 므슴 하료

기이其二

연하煙霞로 집을 삼고 풍월風月로 벗을 사마

태평太平 성대聖代에 병病으로 늘거 가뇌

이 중에 바라는 일은 허믈이나 업고쟈

Twelve songs at Dosan

Lee Hwang

The first half of Dosan[3] twelve songs

The first song

How to do it?
This way or another?
How would it stand
If I behaved like a rustic fool?
What is the cure for this all-consuming longing
To return to nature?

The second song

May the mists and sunsets be my dwelling place,
The winds and moon my only companions.
In a peaceful era under benevolent rule,
I find consolation from the ailments of age.
All I ask from life
Is freedom from shame.

기삼其三

순풍淳風이 죽다 하니 진실眞實로 거즛말이
인성人性이 어지다 하니 진실眞實로 올흔 말이
천하天下에 허다許多 영재英才를 소겨 말슴할가

기사其四

유란幽蘭이 재곡在谷하니 자연自然이 듯디 죠희
백운白雲이 재산在山하니 자연自然이 보디 죠해
이 중에 피미일인彼美一人을 더옥 닛디 못하얘

기오其五

산전山前에 유대有臺하고 대하臺下에 유수有水로다
떼 만흔 갈며기는 오명가명 하거든
엇더타 교교백구皎皎白駒는 멀리 마음 하는고

The third song

It is said that benevolent ways have passed.
Truly, it is a lie!
It is said that human nature is decent—
An undeniable truth!
How then
Can so many prodigies under heaven be deceived?

The fourth song

Shaded orchids in the valley,
Natural virtue of their subtle scent.
White clouds caress the mountainsides,
A joyful balm to the sight.
In the midst of these things,
One more beautiful[4] reigns in my heart!

The fifth song

In front of the mountain there is a small lookout,
Under it there is a river.
Untainted,
A flock of seagulls gliding to and fro.
Why is the wise man's white pony[5]
Drawn to a distant place?[6]

기육其六

춘풍春風에 화만산花滿山하고 추야秋夜에 월만대月滿臺라

사시四時 가흥佳興이 사람과 한가지라

하믈며 어약연비魚躍鳶飛 운영천광雲影天光이야 어늬

  그지 이시리

도산육곡지이 陶山六曲之二

기일其一

천운대天雲臺 도라드러 완락재玩樂齋 소쇄蕭灑한듸

만권萬卷 생애生涯로 낙사樂事 무궁無窮 하얘라

이 중에 왕래往來 풍류風流를 닐러 므슴 할고

The sixth song

The spring breeze disturbs the flowers that coat the
   mountains,
The autumn moon envelops the lookout.
Immersing oneself in the glad recurrence
Of the four seasons.
Is there restraint
For the flying fishes and soaring kites[7] under cloud
   shadow or vibrant sky?

The second half of Dosan twelve songs[8]

The first song

Wandering around the sky-cloud-lookout,
The library of delight appears pristine.
Life with ten thousand books
Provides pleasure without end.
Why even give voice to contentment
With the peripatetic life?

기이其二

뇌정雷霆이 파산破山하여도 농자聾者는 못 듯느니
백일白日이 중천中天하야도 고자瞽者는 못 보느니
우리는 이목총명耳目聰明 남자男子로 농고瞽聾 갓지
  마로리

기삼其三

고인古人도 날 못 보고 나도 고인古人 못 뵈
고인古人를 못 봐도 녀든 길 알픠 잇늬
녀든 길 알픠 잇거든 아니 녀고 엇졀고

기사其四

당시當時에 녀든 길흘 몃 해를 바려두고
어듸 가 단니다가 이제야 도라온고
이제야 도라오나니 년 듸 마음 마로리

The second song

Although the storm breaks upon the mountain,
The deaf cannot hear it.
Although the white sun reaches its zenith,
It is unseen by the blind.
As men with hearing and sight,
We harness our awareness.

The third song

No men of yesteryear have seen me,
Nor I them.
Although I cannot see them,
I know the way they trod.
With this path drawing me on,
How could I deviate from it?

The fourth song

So many lost years,
The way I once trod but then abandoned.
For what have I roamed,
Only to return this late?
Rejoining this faithful path,
I resolve to avoid distractions.

기오其五

청산靑山은 엇졔하여 만고萬古에 프르르며

유수流水는 엇졔하여 주야晝夜애 긋지 아니는고

우리도 그치지 마라 만고상청萬古常靑 하리라

기육其六

우부愚夫도 알며 하거니 그 아니 쉬온가

성인聖人도 못다 하시니 그 아니 어려온가

쉽거나 어렵거나 중에 늙는 줄을 몰래라

『청구영언』

The fifth song

How does the blue mountain
Forever retain its hue?
How does the flowing stream
Course ceaselessly day and night?
Let us forever imitate them,
Changeless pines for all generations.

The sixth song

Even the foolish man believes he understands.
Isn't it easy!
Yet the sage knows his limitations.
Isn't it difficult!
Whether simple or onerous,
I yearn in my learning to be heedless of time.

정철 시조

정철 鄭澈

주문답 酒問答

므슨 일 이루리라 십년十年지이 너를 조차
내 한 일 업시셔 외다 마다 하는이
이제야 절교편絶交篇 지여 전송餞送하되 엇더리

일이나 일우려 하면 처엄에 사괴실가
보면 반기실식 나도 조차 단니드니
진실眞實로 외다옷 하시면 마르신들 아니랴

내 말 고쳐 드러 너 업스면 못 살려니
머흔 일 구즌 일 널로 하여 다 닛거든
이제야 남 괴려 하여 녯 벗 말고 엇지리

Sijo written by Jeong Cheol

Jeong Cheol

Conversation with alcohol

What have I accomplished
Having followed you for ten years?
Whether or not I have done anything wrong
People judge me.
How would it be to compose a letter of divorce
Then bid you farewell in style?

If you wished to accomplish your work,
Why seek my companionship first?
Whenever I catch your eye you seem enthralled,
So I merely follow your lead.
Truly, if you think I do you harm
I care not if we go our separate ways!

Listen to my words again.
I cannot live without you.
Because of you,
I forget all harsh and unpleasant troubles.
How could I cease to be a loyal friend
And pledge my love to another?

무제

내 마음 버혀 내여 뎌 달을 맹글고져
구만리九萬里 장천長天에 번드시 걸려 이셔
고온 님 계신 고듸 가 비최여나 보리라

장진주사 將進酒辭

한 잔盞 먹새그려 또 한 잔盞 먹새그려
곳 것거 산算 노코 무진무진無盡無盡 먹새그려 이 몸
　　주근 후後에 지게 우희 거적 더퍼 주리혀 매여가나
　　유소보장流蘇寶帳에 만인萬人이 우러녜나 어옥새 속
　　새 덥가나무 백양白楊 수페 가기곳 가면 누른 해 흰
　　달 가는 비 굴근 눈 쇼쇼리 바람 불 제 뉘 한 잔盞 먹
　　쟈 할고
하믈며 무덤 우희 잰나비 파람 불 제 뉘우츤들 엇지리

『청구영언』

Untitled

If only I were able to cut out my heart
To make that moon
Immeasurably high in the sky,
Hanging proudly,
I could follow its beam
To find my precious love there[9]

A song for offering rice wine[10]

Let's have a glass of rice wine.
Let's have another!

Let's pluck flowers to record the number of glasses
    and drink without ceasing.
Retiring with my body enfolded in a straw mat,
Fastened to an A-frame to be carried away or borne
    upon a lavish covered bier to be mourned by the
    village,
Then taken to the forest of flame grass, white oak,
    and white poplar.
To rest under the yellow sun, chalk moon, light rain,
    heavy snow or howling wind.
Who will offer me a glass then, for goodness sake!

When the monkey is whistling[11] on your tomb
What use will you have for regret?

방옹시여放翁詩餘

신흠 申欽

산촌山村에 눈이 오니 돌길이 무쳐셰라

시비柴扉를 여지 마라 날 차즈 리 뉘 이시리

밤즁만 일편명월一片明月이 긔 벗인가 하노라

내 가슴 헤친 피로 님의 양자 그려 내여

고당高堂 소벽素壁에 거러 두고 보고 지고

뉘라서 이별離別을 삼겨 사람 죽게 하는고

한식寒食 비 온 밤의 봄빗치 다 퍼졋다

무정無情한 화류花柳도 때를 아라 픠엿거든

엇더타 우리의 님은 가고 아니 오는고

Songs by an exiled old man

Shin Heum

Gravel road of mountain village
Buried in snow.
Do not open the brushwood gate,
For who will visit me?
In the middle of the night,
Only the bright crescent moon for my companion.

Piercing my chest,
Drawing blood for painting my lover's[12] face.
Longing to see his portrait
Hanging on the upper room wall.
Who on earth forces this separation
And leads me to death?

Last night's Hansik[13] rainfall.
The spring mood envelops the world.
Even the heartless flowers and willows
Blossom upon spring's arrival
Why on earth did our beloved go,
Never to return?

어젯밤 비 온 후後에 석류石榴곳이 다 픠엿다
부용芙蓉 당반塘畔에 수정렴水晶簾을 거더 두고
눌 향向한 기픈 시름을 못내 프러 하느뇨

창窓밧긔 워석버석 님이신가 니러 보니
혜란蕙蘭 혜경蹊徑에 낙엽落葉은 므스 일고
어즈버 유한有限한 간장肝腸이 다 그츨가 하노라

은강銀釭에 불 밝고 수로獸爐에 향香이 진지
부용芙蓉 기픈 장帳에 혼자 깨야 안자시니
엇더타 헌사한 져 경점更點아 잠 못 드러 하노라

봄이 왓다 하되 소식消息을 모로더니
냇가에 프른 버들 네 몬져 아도괴야
어스버 인간人間 이별離別을 또 엇지 하느다

노래 삼긴 사람 시름도 하도 할샤
닐러 다 못 닐러 불러나 푸돗든가
진실眞實로 풀릴 거시면은 나도 불러 보리라

『청구영언』

Following last night's rainfall
The pomegranate flowers have fully blossomed.
Rolling up the crystal-beaded blind
To see the lotus pond —
For whom do I long?
And why won't these deep concerns depart?

The crunch of crisp leaves outside the window
   wakes me.
Anticipation of my beloved's return.
Why do the fallen leaves on this orchid pathway
Stir me so?
Alas! This burden
Upon my mortal organs.

From argent lamp, the light shines bright.
The burner's incense pervades the room.
Behind the curtain embroidered with lotus flowers
I sit restlessly in solitude.
Why that frivolous sound of the sleepless clock
Punctuating time?

They say that spring has arrived,
But I cannot feel the season.
Green willow by the brook,
You felt spring's arrival before me.
Alas!
How can I bear this parting from the human realm?

The first man to compose
Was burdened by concerns.
Unable to tell of his disquiet
He relieved it through song.
Truly,
If I could relieve it, I would try to sing!

시조 장르의 정점
The zenith of the sijo genre

어부사시사 漁父四時詞

윤선도 尹善道

춘사春詞

압개예 안개 것고 뒫뫼희 해 비췬다

배 떠라 배 떠라

밤믈은 거의 디고 낟믈이 미러온다

지국총至匊悤 지국총至匊悤 어사와於思臥

강촌江村 온갓 고지 먼 빗치 더옥 됴타

날이 덥도다 믈 우희 고기 떧다

닫 드러라 닫 드러라

갈며기 둘식 세식 오락가락 하느고야

지국총至匊悤 지국총至匊悤 어사와於思臥

낫대는 쥐여 잇다 탁주병濁酒瓶 시럿느냐

Song of a fisherman's four seasons

Yun Seon-do

Spring song

Facing the brook as the fog clears;
The mountain behind bathed in sunlight.
Launch the boat! Launch the boat!
The night's tide recedes,
The day's tide advances.
Ji-go-dok, ji-go-dok, oh-sa-wa.
The flora of the river village
Is better seen by oneself from afar.[14]

Fish swerving and rising,
Drawn to the sun-warmed surface.
Raise the anchor! Raise the anchor!
Seagulls coming and going,
Side by side!
Ji-go-dok, ji-go-dok, oh-sa-wa.
See, I have the fishing rod.
Did you bring the liquor?

동풍東風이 건든 부니 믉결이 고이 닌다

돋 다라라 돋 다라라

동호東湖를 도라보며 서호西湖로 가쟈스라

지국총至匊恩 지국총至匊恩 어사와於思臥

압뫼히 디나가고 뒫뫼히 나아온다

우는 거시 벅구기가 프른 거시 버들숩가

이어라 이어라

어촌漁村 두어 집이 냇 속의 나락들락

지국총至匊恩 지국총至匊恩 어사와於思臥

말가한 기픈 소희 온간 고기 뛰노느다

고은 볏티 쬐얀는듸 믉결이 기름 갓다

이어라 이어라

그믈을 주어 두랴 낙시를 노흘일가

지국총至匊恩 지국총至匊恩 어사와於思臥

탁영가濯纓歌의 흥興이 나니 고기도 니즐로다

East wind blows heedlessly,
Forming ripples on the water.
Raise the sail! Raise the sail!
Looking back at the east lake,
Moving towards the west lake.
Ji-go-dok, ji-go-dok, oh-sa-wa.
Passing the mountains,
Peaks beyond, rising in their stead.

Is that the cuckoo's cry?
Is that the verdant willow forest?
Sail on! Sail on!
A cluster of houses buried in the mist
Flicker in and out of view.
Ji-go-dok, ji-go-dok, oh-sa-wa.
All kinds of fish
Darting, leaping, piercing the crystal depths.

Dappled water beneath beaming sun,
Ripples like oil.
Sail on! Sail on!
Shall I cast the net
Or release the line?
Ji-go-dok, ji-go-dok, oh-sa-wa.
Elated by the old fisherman's song,
I have forgotten to fish!

석양夕陽이 빗겨시니 그만하야 도라가쟈

돋 디여라 돋 디여라

안류岸柳 정화汀花는 고븨고븨 새롭고야

지국총至匊悤 지국총至匊悤 어사와於思臥

삼공三公을 불리소냐 만사萬事를 생각하랴

방초芳草를 발와 보며 난지蘭芷도 뜨더 보쟈

배 셰여라 배 셰여라

일엽一葉 편주扁舟에 시른 거시 므스 것고

지국총至匊悤 지국총至匊悤 어사와於思臥

갈 제는 내뿐이오 올 제는 달이로다

취醉하야 누언다가 여흘 아래 나리려다

배 매여라 배 매여라

낙홍落紅이 흘러오니 도원桃源이 갓갑도다

지국총至匊悤 지국총至匊悤 어사와於思臥

인세人世 홍진紅塵이 언메나 가렷느니

The sunset sinks into the earth.
Let us cease and retire.
Lower the sail! Lower the sail!
Pristine willows and flowers on the riverbank
Astonish with their vibrancy.
Ji-go-dok, ji-go-dok, oh-sa-wa.
Why envy the three eminent statesmen?
Why have such concerns?

Looking back at the flower-strewn grass,
I shall gather orchids.
Stop the boat! Stop the boat!
What should I carry
On this delicate boat?
Ji-go-dok, ji-go-dok, oh-sa-wa.
I set sail alone.
Now returning, the moon accompanies me.

Woken from a merry slumber,
I attempt to disembark.
Moor the boat! Moor the boat!
Floating peach tree petals
Pointing me to the secluded garden.
Ji-go-dok, ji-go-dok, oh-sa-wa.
Yet how the dust of the human realm
Obscures my view!

낙시줄 거더 노코 봉창蓬窓의 달을 보쟈

달 디여라 달 디여라

하마 밤 들거냐 자규子規 소리 맑게 난다

지국총至匊恩 지국총至匊恩 어사와於思臥

나믄 흥興이 무궁無窮하니 갈 길흘 니젓딴다

내일來日이 또 업스랴 봄밤이 몃 덜 새리

배 브텨라 배 브텨라

낫대로 막대 삼고 시비柴扉를 차자 보쟈

지국총至匊恩 지국총至匊恩 어사와於思臥

어부漁父 생애生涯는 이렁구리 디낼로다

Let's put away the fishing line
And watch the moon from the bedroom window.
Stow the anchor! Stow the anchor!
Has night descended already?
The scope owl's trill pierces the crisp air.
Ji-go-dok, ji-go-dok, oh-sa-wa.
Through my boundless exuberance
I have lost my way!

Will there not be another tomorrow?
More spring nights lie ahead.
Beach the boat! Beach the boat!
Make my staff a fishing rod
And return to the brushwood gate.
Ji-go-dok, ji-go-dok, oh-sa-wa.
In such a life
The fisherman passes his days.

하사夏詞

구즌비 머저 가고 시냇믈이 맑아 온다
배 떠라 배 떠라
낫대를 두러메니 기픈 흥興을 금禁 못할돠
지국총至匊悤 지국총至匊悤 어사와於思臥
연강煙江 첩장疊嶂은 뉘라셔 그려낸고

년닙희 밥 싸 두고 반찬으란 쟝만 마라
닫 드러라 닫 드러라
청약립靑蒻笠은 써 잇노라 녹사의綠蓑衣 가져오냐
지국총至匊悤 지국총至匊悤 어사와於思臥
무심無心한 백구白鷗는 내 좃는가 제 좃는가

마람닙희 바람 나니 봉창蓬窓이 서늘코야
돋 다라라 돋 다라라
녀름 바람 뎡할소냐 가는 대로 배 시겨라
지국총至匊悤 지국총至匊悤 어사와於思臥
북포北浦 남강南江이 어듸 아니 됴흘러니

Summer song

The punishing rain eases,
The brook becomes clear.
Launch the boat! Launch the boat!
Carrying the fishing rod on my shoulder,
I cannot refrain from deep exuberance.
Ji-go-dok, ji-go-dok, oh-sa-wa.
Whose hand has drawn
This mist-shrouded river and these jagged peaks?

Wrap the rice with the lotus leaves
And do not prepare the side dishes.
Raise the anchor! Raise the anchor!
I'm wearing my blue bamboo hat.
Did you bring my green straw raincoat?[15]
Ji-go-dok, ji-go-dok, oh-sa-wa.
The indifferent white seagulls,
Do they follow me? Or do I follow them?

The wind caresses the algae.
A chill penetrates the window.
Raise the sail! Raise the sail!
Summer wind is undiscerning.
Let the boat sail wherever the wind takes her.
Ji-go-dok, ji-go-dok, oh-sa-wa.
What does it matter
Whether I go to the north lake or the south river?

맑결이 흐리거든 발을 싯다 엇더하리

이어라 이어라

오강吳江의 가쟈 하니 천년노도千年怒濤 슬플로다

지국총至匊悤 지국총至匊悤 어사와於思臥

초강楚江의 가쟈 하니 어복충혼魚腹忠魂 낟글셰라

만류녹음萬柳綠陰 어릔 고듸 일편태기一片苔磯 기특
   奇特하다

이어라 이어라

다리예 다듣거든 어인쟁도漁人爭渡 허믈 마라

지국총至匊悤 지국총至匊悤 어사와於思臥

학발노옹鶴髮老翁 만나거든 뇌택양거雷澤讓居 효칙效則
   하쟈

If the lake were muddy,

Who would care whether I washed my feet.[16]

Sail on! Sail on!

I meant to visit Wu River,

But the raging waves of a thousand years saddened
my heart.[17]

Ji-go-dok, ji-go-dok, oh-sa-wa.

I meant to visit Chu River

But feared catching the fishes holding that loyal
subject's soul.[18]

Where the shadow of the willow forest falls,

A fragment of moss clings to one arresting pebble.

Sail on! Sail on!

When you arrive at the bridge

Don't blame the fishermen who jostle to cross it
first.

Ji-go-dok, ji-go-dok, oh-sa-wa.

When meeting a white-haired man

Let's follow the ways of old and yield our place.

긴 날이 져므는 줄 흥興의 미쳐 모르도다

돋 디여라 돋 디여라

뱃대를 두드리고 수조가水調歌를 블러 보쟈

지국총至匊恩 지국총至匊恩 어사와於思臥

애내성欸乃聲 중中에 만고심萬古心을 긔 뉘 알고

석양夕陽이 됴타마는 황혼黃昏이 갓갑거다

배 셰여라 배 셰여라

바회 우희 에구븐 길 솔 아래 빗겨 잇다

지국총至匊恩 지국총至匊恩 어사와於思臥

벽수碧樹 앵성鶯聲이 곧곧이 들리느다

몰래 우희 그믈 널고 둠 미틔 누어 쉬쟈

배 매여라 배 매여라

모괴를 밉다 하랴 창승蒼蠅과 엇더하니

지국총至匊恩 지국총至匊恩 어사와於思臥

다만 한 근심은 상대부桑大夫 드르려다

Lost in my exuberance,
Late to notice the close of day.
Lower the sail! Lower the sail!
Let's beat on the side of the boat
And sing a song on the water.
Ji-go-dok, ji-go-dok, oh-sa-wa.
The song and the oars resound.
Who can know my aged heart?

The sunset captivates me,
Yet signals twilit hours.
Stop the boat! Stop the boat!
The path winding around the rocks
Slopes down below the pine trees.
Ji-go-dok, ji-go-dok, oh-sa-wa.
The oriole's song echoes
Throughout the green forest.

Let's spread the net on the sand
And rest under the canopy of the boat.
Moor the boat! Moor the boat!
If I say I hate mosquitoes,
How much more a blue bottle fly?[19]
Ji-go-dok, ji-go-dok, oh-sa-wa.
My sole concern
Is being overheard by Sang the Courtier.[20]

밤 사이 풍랑風浪을 미리 어이 짐쟉하리

닫 디여라 닫 디여라

야도野渡 횡주橫舟를 뉘라셔 닐럿는고

지국총至匊悤 지국총至匊悤 어사와於思臥

간변澗邊 유초幽草도 진실眞實로 어엳브다

와실蝸室을 바라보니 백운白雲이 둘러 잇다

배 븟뎌라 배 븟뎌라

부들부체 가르 쥐고 석경石逕으로 올라가쟈

지국총至匊悤 지국총至匊悤 어사와於思臥

어옹漁翁이 한가閑暇터냐 이거시 구실이라

I could not have foretold
The coming of the storm during the night.
Stow the anchor! Stow the anchor!
I recall a poem about a neglected boat
Drifting idly at a desolate landing stage.
Ji-go-dok, ji-go-dok, oh-sa-wa.
Delicate scent of the grass covering the riverbank
Is truly agreeable to me.

I look up at my tiny shelter
Brushed by white clouds.
Beach the boat! Beach the boat!
Let's climb up the rocky pass,
Grasping the straw fan.
Ji-go-dok, ji-go-dok, oh-sa-wa.
If anyone would call this fisherman idle,
This will be his defence.

추사秋詞

물외物外예 조흔 일이 어부생애漁父生涯 아니러냐

배 떠라 배 떠라

어옹漁翁을 욷디 마라 그림마다 그렷더라

지국총至匊恖 지국총至匊恖 어사와於思臥

사시흥四時興이 한가지나 추강秋江이 읃듬이라

수국水國의 가을히 드니 고기마다 살져 읻다

닫 드러라 닫 드러라

만경萬頃 징파澄波의 슬카지 용여容與하쟈

지국총至匊恖 지국총至匊恖 어사와於思臥

인간人間을 도라보니 머도록 더옥 됴타

백운白雲이 니러나고 나모 긋티 흐느긴다

돋 다라라 돋 다라라

밀믈의 서호西湖오 혈믈의 동호東湖 가쟈

지국총至匊恖 지국총至匊恖 어사와於思臥

백빈白蘋 홍료紅蓼는 곳마다 경景이로다

Autumn song

Isn't a fisherman's life idyllic,
Far from worldly concerns?
Launch the boat! Launch the boat!
Don't laugh at old fishermen,
They appear in every watercolour.
Ji-go-dok, ji-go-dok, oh-sa-wa.
The four seasons' scenes fill me with exuberance,
But none more so than the autumn river.

Autumn has arrived to this water-world.
The fish are fattening.
Raise the anchor! Raise the anchor!
Let's ride the endless furrows of crystal wavelets,
Savour the pleasure until we exhaust it.
Ji-go-dok, ji-go-dok, oh-sa-wa.
Looking back at the human world —
The further away the better!

The white clouds have risen;
The edge of the bough is weeping.
Raise the sail! Raise the sail!
With the flood tide we will go to the west lake,
With the ebbing tide to the east lake.
Ji-go-dok, ji-go-dok, oh-sa-wa.
Wherever I go,
White smartweed and scarlet water flowers provide
    a vibrant scene.

그러기 떳는 밧긔 못 보던 뫼 뵈느고야

이어라 이어라

낙시질도 하려니와 취取한 거시 이 흥興이라

지국총至匊悤 지국총至匊悤 어사와於思臥

석양夕陽이 바의니 천산千山이 금수錦繡로다

은순銀脣 옥척玉尺이 몃치나 걸렫느니

이어라 이어라

노화蘆花의 블 부러 갈희야 구어 노코

지국총至匊悤 지국총至匊悤 어사와於思臥

딜병을 거후리혀 박구기예 브어 다고

녑바람이 고이 부니 다론 돋긔 도라와다

돋 디여라 돋 디여라

명색暝色은 나아오듸 청흥清興은 머러 읻다

지국총至匊悤 지국총至匊悤 어사와於思臥

홍수紅樹 청강清江이 슬믜디도 아니한다

I see a mountain unveiled
In the distance where the wild geese are hovering.
Sail on! Sail on!
Fishing gives pleasure,
Yet I continue basking in this exuberance.
Ji-go-dok, ji-go-dok, oh-sa-wa.
When the sunset is shimmering
The thousand mountains are as embroidered silk.

How many treasured silver-mouthed fish
Have I caught?
Sail on! Sail on!
Set the reed straws alight
And roast the fish.
Ji-go-dok, ji-go-dok, oh-sa-wa.
Tilt the clay bottle
And pour the rice wine into the ladle.

The gentle breeze caresses my side
And blows into the raised sail.
Lower the sail! Lower the sail!
The sky is darkening
And the exuberance that the idyll inspired is
    subsiding.
Ji-go-dok, ji-go-dok, oh-sa-wa.
Vermilion-hued leaves beside the clear river
Could never fatigue me.

흰 이슬 빈견는듸 발근 달 도다 온다

배 셰여라 배 셰여라

봉황루鳳凰樓 묘연渺然하니 청광淸光을 눌을 줄고

지국총至匊恖 지국총至匊恖 어사와於思臥

옥토玉兎의 띤는 약藥을 호객豪客을 먹이고쟈

건곤乾坤이 제곰인가 이거시 어드메오

배 매여라 배 매여라

서풍진西風塵 몯 미츠니 부체하야 머엇 하리

지국총至匊恖 지국총至匊恖 어사와於思臥

드론 말이 업서시니 귀 시서 머엇 하리

White dew glistens as it trickles down the grassy bank.
The bright moon rises above.
Stop the boat! Stop the boat!
The royal court lies far beyond;
To whom can I give this clear moonlight?
Ji-go-dok, ji-go-dok, oh-sa-wa.
A jade hare on the moon pounds out the medicine.[21]
I yearn to give it to a great man.

Are heaven and earth indifferent to each other?
Where do I find myself?
Moor the boat! Moor the boat!
Dust of the west wind has not yet arrived.
What use is it then to wave a fan?
Ji-go-dok, ji-go-dok, oh-sa-wa.
Since I have heard nothing,
What would it profit me to wash my ears?[22]

옷 우희 서리 오듸 치운 줄을 모를로다

닫 디여라 닫 디여라

조선釣船이 좁다 하나 부세浮世과 얻더하니

지국총至匊悤 지국총至匊悤 어사와於思臥

내일도 이리하고 모뢰도 이리하쟈

송간松間 석실石室의 가 효월曉月을 보쟈 하니

배 브텨라 배 브텨라

공산空山 낙엽落葉의 길흘 엇디 아라볼고

지국총至匊悤 지국총至匊悤 어사와於思臥

백운白雲이 좃차오니 여라의女蘿衣 므겁고야

Frost has fallen on my clothing
But the chill does not affect me.
Stow the anchor! Stow the anchor!
A fishing boat is a modest craft,
Yet, is this life not superior to the mundane world?
Ji-go-dok, ji-go-dok, oh-sa-wa.
Let's live like this
Tomorrow and the day after.

I intended to ascend to the pines-embraced hermitage
To watch the dawn moon.
Beach the boat! Beach the boat!
How can I discern the way that is concealed
By fallen leaves in this empty mountain?
Ji-go-dok, ji-go-dok, oh-sa-wa.
A white cloud[23] pursues me.
My hemp robe weighs heavily upon me.

동사冬詞

구룸 거든 후의 핻빋치 두텁거다
배 떠라 배 떠라
천지天地 폐색閉塞호듸 바다흔 의구依舊하다
지국총至匊悤 지국총至匊悤 어사와於思臥
가업슨 믉결이 깁 편 듯 하어 잇다

주대 다스리고 뱃밥을 박안느냐
닫 드러라 닫 드러라
소상瀟湘 동정洞庭은 그믈이 언다 한다
지국총至匊悤 지국총至匊悤 어사와於思臥
이때에 어조漁釣하기 이만한 듸 업도다

여튼 갣 고기들히 먼 소희 다 갇느니
돈 다라라 돈 다라라
져근덛 날 됴흔 제 바탕의 나가 보쟈
지국총至匊悤 지국총至匊悤 어사와於思臥
밋기 곧다오면 굴근 고기 믄다 한다

Winter song

After the clouds have cleared,
The sunlight caresses the earth with its
    benevolence.
Launch the boat! Launch the boat!
Heaven and earth have been frozen shut
But the sea remains the same.
Ji-go-dok, ji-go-dok, oh-sa-wa.
Boundless waves
Resemble smooth silk unwound.

Are rod and line prepared?
Is the boat caulked?
Raise the anchor! Raise the anchor!
They say the net freezes
On Xiaoxiang River and Dongting Lake.24
Ji-go-dok, ji-go-dok, oh-sa-wa.
Nowhere surpasses this place
For fishing at this time.

The fishes of the shallow coast
Have swum into the distant waters.
Raise the sail! Raise the sail!
Soon the weather will be ideal.
Let's head to the sea.
Ji-go-dok, ji-go-dok, oh-sa-wa.
If the bait is enticing,
The large fishes will bite.

간밤의 눈 갠 후後에 경물景物이 달랃고야

이어라 이어라

압희는 만경유리萬頃琉璃 뒤희는 천첩옥산千疊玉山

지국총至匊悤 지국총至匊悤 어사와於思臥

선계仙界인가 불계佛界인가 인간人間이 아니로다

그믈 낙시 니저 두고 뱃젼을 두드린다

이어라 이어라

압개를 건너고쟈 몃 번이나 혜여 본고

지국총至匊悤 지국총至匊悤 어사와於思臥

무단無端한 된바람이 행혀 아니 부러올까

자라 가는 가마괴 몃 낫치 디나거니

돋 디여라 돋 디여라

압길히 어두우니 모셜暮雪이 자자뎠다

지국총至匊悤 지국총至匊悤 어사와於思臥

아압지鵝鴨池를 뉘 텨셔 초목참草木慚을 싯돋던고

Last night's snowfall now cleared away;
A landscape transformed!
Sail on! Sail on!
Ahead of me, manifold translucent waves,
Behind me, countless jade green mountains.
Ji-go-dok, ji-go-dok, oh-sa-wa.
Is this a fairy land or nirvana?
Surely it is not the human world!

I forget about the net and rod,
Tapping instead on the boat's bow.
Sail on! Sail on!
How many times have I thought
About crossing the water before me?
Ji-go-dok, ji-go-dok, oh-sa-wa.
I fear the harsh winds[25]
Stirring unprovoked.

How many flocks of crows seeking their sleep
Have passed above?
Lower the sail! Lower the sail!
The road ahead has darkened,
The evening snow is falling faster.
Ji-go-dok, ji-go-dok, oh-sa-wa.
Who will remove this shame which even the forest
    feels?
Who will beat the pond of ducks?[26]

단애丹崖 취벽翠壁이 화병畵屛간티 둘럿는듸

배 셰여라 배 셰여라

거구巨口 세린細鱗을 낟그나 몯 낟그나

지국총至匊悤 지국총至匊悤 어사와於思臥

고주孤舟 사립簑笠에 흥興 계워 안잣노라

믉가의 외로온 솔 혼자 어이 싁싁한고

배 매여라 배 매여라

머흔 구룸 한恨티 마라 세상世上을 가리온다

지국총至匊悤 지국총至匊悤 어사와於思臥

파랑성波浪聲을 염厭티 마라 진훤塵喧을 막는또다

The red cliff and the green rocks,
Surround the lake like a painted screen.
Stop the boat! Stop the boat!
I am indifferent to the success of
Catching the prized fish.
Ji-go-dok, ji-go-dok, oh-sa-wa.
Sitting in this lonely boat, wearing humble attire,
Losing myself in elation.

How persistently it stands alone,
A solitary pine tree on the shore.
Moor the boat! Moor the boat!
Do not lament the dense clouds.
They obscure the mundane world.
Ji-go-dok, ji-go-dok, oh-sa-wa.
Do not despise the roar of the waves.
They obscure agitations brought by vexing dust.

창주滄洲 오도吾道를 녜브터 닐럳더라

닫 디여라 닫 디여라

칠리七里 여흘 양피羊皮 옷슨 긔 얻더하 니런고

지국총至匊悤 지국총至匊悤 어사와於思臥

삼천육백三千六百 낙시질은 손고븐 제 엇디턴고

어와 져므러 간다 연식宴息이 맏당토다

배 븟뎌라 배 븟뎌라

가는 눈 쁘린 길 블근 곳 훗더딘 듸 흥치며 거러가셔

지국총至匊悤 지국총至匊悤 어사와於思臥

설월雪月이 서봉西峰의 넘도록 송창松窓을 비겨 잇쟈

『고산유고』

From ages past, people have praised
'Our way of life in Cangzhou.'[27]
Stow the anchor! Stow the anchor!
What kind of man was he
Who wore a sheepskin covering and fished at Qili
   River?[28]
Ji-go-dok, ji-go-dok, oh-sa-wa.
What was it like for Lyu shang
Fishing for ten years, anticipating the ideal king?[29]

Oh my! The day is drawing to a close.
Time to rest after a welcome repast.
Beach the boat! Beach the boat!
A scattering of snow on the path with red flowers
   interspersed,
I make my way home jubilantly.
Ji-go-dok, ji-go-dok, oh-sa-wa.
I will lean against the pine tree window[30]
Until the winter moon passes over the western
   peak.

3부
Part 3

사대부들의 전원 시조

Pastoral sijo of Neo-Confucian literati

전원사시가 田園四時歌

춘春

봄날이 졈졈 기니 잔설殘雪이 다 녹거다
매화梅花는 발셔 디고 버들가지 누르럿다
아희야 울 잘 고티고 채전菜田 갈게 하야라

양파陽坡의 플이 기니 봄빗치 느저 잇다
소원小園 도화桃花는 밤비예 다 피거다
아희야 쇼 됴히 머겨 논밭 갈게 하야라

Pastoral songs of the four seasons

Shin Gye-young

Spring

Spring days are gradually lengthening,
The last of the snow has melted away.
The plum tree flowers have already fallen.
The willow branches have yellowed.
Boy, repair the fence,
Then we shall furrow the vegetable field.

Grass still growing on the sun-drenched hill —
Late spring's persistence.
Peach flowers in the small garden,
Brought to full blossom by the night's rain.
Boy, give the cow a full feed,
Then furrow the fields.

하夏

잔화殘花 다 딘 후後의 녹음綠陰이 기퍼 간다

백일白日 고촌孤村에 낫닭의 소릐로다

아희야 계면됴 불러라 긴 조롬 깨오쟈

원림園林 적막寂寞한듸 북창北窓을 빗겨시니

거문고 노라라 낫잠을 깨와괴야

-종장 유실-

추秋

흰 이슬 서리 되니 가을이 느저 잇다

긴 들 황운黃雲이 한 빗치 피거고야

아희야 비즌 술 걸러라 추흥秋興 계워 하노라

동리東籬에 국화菊花 피니 중양重陽이 거에로다

자채自綵로 비즌 술이 하마 아니 니것느냐

아희야 자해황계紫蟹黃鷄로 안주酒 작만 하야라

Summer

Late flowers have fallen,
The green forest has darkened.
Lonely village beneath the scorching sun.
The afternoon sound of hens clucking.
Boy, sing Gyemyon-jo,[31]
So I may shed this drowsiness.

The garden is tranquil
As I lean against the north window.
Play the geomungo[32]
To help me wake up.

[N.B. The last two lines of this stanza have been lost.]

Autumn

Clear dew has turned to frost,
Autumn is now at its height.
Golden sea of rice
Flourishes in the long field.
Boy! Filter the liquor from the rice.
How this autumn jubilation takes hold of me!

Chrysanthemums blossoming at the east fence
Jungyang[33] is almost upon us.
The wine made of the finest rice grains
Has ripened already, hasn't it?
Boy, take the prime crab and chicken
And prepare ample side dishes.

동冬

북풍北風이 노피 부니 앞 뫼희 눈이 딘다
모첨茅簷 찬 빗치 석양夕陽이 거에로다
아희야 두죽豆粥 니것느냐 먹고 자라 하로라

어제 쇼 친 구들 오늘이야 채 덥거니
긴 잠 계우 깨니 아젹 날이 놉파 잇다
아희야 서리 녹앗느냐 닐고 쟈고 하노라

제석除夕

이바 아희들아 새해 온다 즐겨 마라
헌서한 세월歲月이 소년少年 아사 가느니라
우리도 새해 즐겨하다가 이 백발白髮이 되얏노라

이바 아희들아 날 샌다 깃거 마라
자고 새고 자고 새니 세월歲月이 몃츳 가리
백년百年이 하 초초草草하니 나는 굿버 하노라

『선석유고』

Winter

North wind blows from afar.
Snow falls on the mountain before me.
Cold light strokes the eaves of the thatched house,
Sunset approaches.
Boy, has the bean porridge boiled yet?
I wish to eat then sleep.

The ondol[34] that was lit yesterday
Emits scant heat today.
Half awake having overslept,
The sun is now high.
Boy, did the frost melt?
I wish to return to sleep.

New Year's Eve

Hey boys!
Don't look forward to the coming New Year!
The passing of energetic time
Will steal away your youth.
The enjoyment of past New Year festivities
Now replaced with this white hair.

Hey boys!
Don't be too excited about the dawning New Year.
Sleep and awaken, sleep and awaken.
How many days in a lifetime?
A hundred years fly past
And I lament.

전가팔곡田家八曲

이휘일 李徽逸

원풍願豊

세상世上의 바린 몸이 견무畎畝의 늘거 가니

밧겻일 내 모르고 하는 일 무스 일고

이 중中의 우국성심憂國誠心은 연풍年豊을 원願하노라

춘春

농인農人이 와 이로듸 봄 왓늬 바틔 가새

압집의 쇼보 잡고 뒷집의 따보 내늬

두어라 내 집 부듸 하랴 남 하니 더욱 됴타

Eight pastoral songs

Lee Hwi-il

A wish for a good year

Abandoned by the world,
Growing older by the furrowed field.
What am I doing
By forsaking worldly things?
In the midst of this life, concern for the country
    grips me —
I yearn for a rich harvest.

Spring

A farmer comes by saying,
'Spring is here at last. Let's head to the field.'
Borrow the plough frame and hoe
From the neighbour.
Hold on! Why start with my field?
Better to begin with another's.

하夏

여름날 더운 적의 단 따히 부리로다

밧고랑 매쟈 하니 땀 흘너 따희 듯네

어사와 입립신고粒粒辛苦 어늬 분이 알으실고

추秋

가을희 곡셕 보니 됴흠도 됴흘셰고

내 힘의 닐운 거시 머거도 마시로다

이 밧긔 천사만종千駟萬鍾을 부러 무슴 하리오

동冬

밤의란 사츨 꼬고 나죄란 뛰를 부여

초가草家집 자바매고 농기農器 졈 차려스라

내년來年희 봄 온다 하거든 결의 종사縱事 하리라

Summer

During the sweltering summer's day
The ground is heated like fire.
Trying to make furrows,
My sweat pours down upon the earth.
Alas! Who appreciates this toiling for growth,
Grain by grain?

Autumn

Seeing these crops in autumn
My spirits rise.
My efforts in the field
Find their reward in this welcome repast.
Being content,
Why envy the emperor's carriages and salaried
    aristocracy?

Winter

Twining the straw all night,
In the daytime cutting the thatch.
Tying the cottage roof
And preparing the farming equipment.
I am reminded that spring will return next year.
I will set to it at once.

신晨

새배빗 나쟈나셔 백설百舌이 소릐한다
일거라 아희들아 밧 보러 가쟈스라
밤 사이 이슬 긔운에 언마나 기런는고 하노라

오午

보리밥 지어 담고 도트랏 갱을 하여
배골는 농부農夫들을 진시趁時예 머겨스라
아희야 한 그릇 올녀라 친親히 맛바 보내리라

석夕

서산西山애 해 지고 플긋테 이슬 난다
호뮈를 둘너메고 달 듸여 가쟈스라
이 중中의 즐거운 뜻을 닐러 무슴 하리오

『저곡전가팔곡필첩』

Dawn

Before the dawn light comes
Hundreds of mouths yell:
'Wake up, boys!
Let's go to the field
To check how the crops have grown
With the night's dew.'

Afternoon

Making barley rice,
Serving acorn curd soup.
Make haste
To feed the famished farmers.
Boy! Dish out a bowl for me.
Let me taste it first.

Evening

The sun is setting behind the west mountain,
Dew is forming on the blades of grass.
I carry a hand hoe over my shoulder.
Let us return home accompanied by lunar light.
In the midst of this pastoral life
Why give voice to my elation?

기생과 중인 남성 가객들의 시조

Sijo written by Kisaeng and middle-class male singers

황진이 시조

황진이 黃眞伊

무제

청산리青山裏 벽계수碧溪水야 수이 감을 쟈랑 마라

일도一到 창해滄海 하면 도라오기 어려오니

명월明月이 만공산滿空山하니 수여 간들 엇더리

무제

동지冬至달 기나긴 밤을 한허리를 버혀 내여

춘풍春風 니불 아레 서리서리 너헛다가

어론 님 오신 날 밤이여든 구뷔구뷔 펴리라

Sijo written by Hwang Jin-i

Hwang Jin-i

Untitled

Jade green brook[35] enclosed within blue mountain,
Do not boast of your rapid flow.
Once you reach the sea's great expanse
You will struggle to return.
Now that the bright moon enfolds the empty
    mountain,
Why not set aside your burdens and find solace
    with me?

Untitled

I will carve in half
The waist of the winter solstice night,
Pad the spring breeze quilt
With nocturnal hours.
I will unroll it
On the night of my beloved's return.

무제

어져 내 일이야 그릴 줄을 모로드냐
이시라 하더면 가랴마는 제 구틔야
보내고 그리는 정情은 나도 몰라 하노라

『청구영언』

무제

청산靑山은 내 뜻이오 녹수綠水는 님의 정情이
녹수綠水 흘너간들 청산靑山이야 변變할손가
녹수綠水도 청산靑山을 못 니져 우러 예어 가는고

『대동풍아』

무제

내 언제 신信이 업셔 님을 언제 소겻관듸
월침月沈 삼경三更에 온 뜻지 전全혀 업늬
추풍秋風에 지는 닙 소릐야 낸들 어이 하리오

『동가선』

Untitled

Alas, what have I done!
Where was the inkling that I would miss him so?
If I had insisted that he stayed
He would not have left me.
I, myself permitted his departure
That caused this bitter longing.

Untitled

The blue mountain is my loyalty,
The green water is my beloved's love.
Though the green water flows away,
How could the blue mountain change?
The green water cannot forget the blue mountain.
And why wouldn't it flow away, weeping?

Untitled

What cause did I give you
To expect me to appear?
I never meant for you to believe
That I would disturb the fallen leaves at midnight.
Why blame me?
It is the autumn wind that influences your delusion.

김천택 시조

김천택 金天澤

무제

영욕榮辱이 병행並行하니 부귀富貴도 불관不關트라

제일第一 강산江山에 내 혼자 님자 되야

석양夕陽에 낙싯대 두러메고 오명가명 하리라

무제

전원田園에 나믄 흥興을 전나귀에 모도 싯고

계산溪山 니근 길로 흥치며 도라와셔

아희 금서琴書를 다스려라 나믄 해를 보내리라

Sijo written by Kim Cheon-taek

Kim Cheon-taek

Untitled

Both honour and humiliation are familiar to me,
I have no care for riches or nobility.
Residing among these incomparable rivers and
    mountains
As though a landlord,
Tilting the fishing rod over my shoulder,
Free to wander from place to place.

Untitled

Jubilant in the field
I load the supplies on the donkey, my companion.
I return through this familiar ravine
With elation.
Boy! Hand me the geomungo music score.
I will play during the remaining day-lit hours.

무제

운소雲霄에 오로젼들 나래 업시 어이하며
봉도蓬島로 가쟈 하니 주즙舟楫을 어이하리
찰하리 산림山林에 주인主人 되야 이 세계世界를
　니즈리라

무제

녹이상제綠駬霜蹄 역상櫪上에셔 늙고 용천설악
　龍泉雪鍔 갑리匣裏에 운다
장부丈夫의 혜온 뜻을 속졀업시 못 이로고
귀밋테 흰 털이 날니니 글을 셜워 하노라

『청구영언』

Untitled

Even if I wished to climb up to the sky shrouded by
    the clouds,
How could I do it without wings?
Even if I desired to retreat to a sacred island,
How could I afford a ship?
I'd rather be an owner of a mountain forest
And forget this mundane world.

Untitled

An incomparable racehorse ages in the stall,
A legendary sword cries inside the sheath.
I have failed to live up to the valorous will
Of the gentleman.
White hair beneath my ears flutters
As I lament the wasted years.

박효관 시조

박효관 朴孝寬

무제

공산空山에 우는 졉동 너는 어이 우지는다
너도 날과 갓치 무음 이별離別 하엿느냐
아무리 피나게 운들 대답對答이나 하더냐

무제

꿈에 왓던 님이 깨여 보니 간듸업늬
탐탐耽耽이 괴던 사랑 날 바리고 어듸 간고
꿈속이 허사虛事라만정 쟈로 뵈게 하여라

Sijo written by Park Hyo-gwan

Park Hyo-gwan

Untitled

Jeopdong bird,[36] crying in the empty mountain,
Why are you wailing?
Just like me,
Did you depart from your lover?
No matter how bitterly you spewed blood,
Did your lover ever answer?

Untitled

As I awaken, my lover who came to me in my
    dream
Is nowhere to be found.
Expressing his love intimately, only to abandon me.
Why did he depart?
I know a dream is illusory,
But let it recur.

무제

님 글인 상사몽相思夢이 실솔蟋蟀의 넉시 되야
추야장秋夜長 깊푼 밤에 님의 방房에 드럿다가
날 닛고 집히 든 잠을 깨와 볼가 하노라

무제

동군東君이 도라오니 만물萬物이 개자락皆自樂을
초목草木 곤충昆虫들은 해해마다 회생回生커늘
사람은 어인 연고緣故로 귀불귀歸不歸를 하는고

무제

서리 티고 별 성귄 제 울며 가는 져 기럭아
네 길이 그 언마나 밧바 밤길 좃차 녜는 것가
강남江南에 기약期約을 두엇시믜 늦져 갈가 져혜라

『가곡원류』

Untitled

My lovesick dream
Transforms me into the soul of a cricket.
During a protracted autumn night,
I will invade my lover's chamber.
Breaking
Deep forgetful sleep.

Untitled

With the return of spring,
Every creature is reinvigorated.
Grass, trees, and insects
Revitalised year by year.
Why cannot man return
Once he has gone?

Untitled

Wild goose in a sky with few stars.
Tears falling upon the frost below.
Such haste to make your journey,
Flying even through the night!
'I promised to migrate south of the river[37]
And fear arriving too late.'

Endnotes

1　Makkoli is a traditional Korean cloudy rice wine that is popular with the common people.

2　The trope of the white seagull symbolises innocence. It was believed that this bird had the ability to detect whether or not a person was indifferent to worldly desire.

3　Dosan is the place to which the poet retreated in his 60s.

4　'One more beautiful' refers to the king in the court. It is an old literary convention to refer to a king as a beautiful woman.

5　This is a reference to the Chinese classic *Si-ching* (*The Book of Poetry*). The title of one of the poems in this anthology translates as 'The White Pony', which is ridden by wise men.

6　The distant place refers to the king's palace in Hanyang (modernday Seoul).

7　Everything in nature has its place and its destiny to follow, from the passing of the seasons to the activities of creatures, to lightness and darkness. The 'flying fishes and soaring kites' is another reference to the *Si-ching*.

8　The first half of this song conveys Lee Hwang's will to live in harmony with nature as a hermit. In the second half of the song he specifies the way to achieve this, which is to devote himself to lifelong study.

9   Jeong Cheol expresses his love and loyalty toward the king whom he is calling 'my precious love'.

10 This sijo is called Saseol sijo, which means that its lyrics are significantly longer than those of normal sijo.

11 A monkey's whistling would cause a poet of this time to become melancholy. The reason for this was that in China when courtiers were banished from the court, which was located in the north, they were sent to the south, where they would encounter exotic monkeys. This animal reminded the poet of the reality of the solitude that he experienced in his state of exile.

12 In this poem, the 'lover' may refer to the late King Seonjo. However, since the poem was written during King Gwanghae's reign, this was potentially dangerous.

13 Falling on the 105th day from the winter solstice, Hansik, which literally means 'cold rice', is one of the subdivisions of the seasons. There is a famous story about the origin of Hansik. In China, there was a king who was fleeing some rebels with his subordinates. When he was starving, a loyal subordinate whose name was Jie Zitui (Gaejachu in Korean) cut his thigh and fed the king. When the king was restored to his throne, he forgot this loyal subordinate, which resulted in Jie Zitui hiding himself in the mountain. When the king realised his oversight and called him, he would not come out from the mountain. The king ordered his men to set fire to the trees on this mountain in order to force him out, however, Jie Zitui chose to burn to death. In memory of his loyalty, it is said that people started to prohibit the use of fire and began the practice of eating cold rice on this day.

14 'Song of a fisherman's four seasons' has an unusual form for sijo. In all other sijo, the syllabic number pattern of the last line differs from the first and second lines which fall on a 3-4-3-

4 syllabic number pattern. However, in this sijo Yun Seon-do persists with the same pattern until the last line and between the lines there are two auxiliary phrases which enhance the speaker's sense of exuberance. The first one, indicating the movement of the boat, 'Launch the boat! Launch the boat!', comes between lines one and two. This auxiliary phrase changes according to the stanza. The second one, 'Ji-go-dok, ji-go-dok, oh-sa-wa', is an onomatopoeia of rowing with oars. This phrase is repeated in every stanza. Despite the formal modification, his song is traditionally regarded as the most sophisticated sijo of all. At the very end of the fortieth stanza, he keeps the metrical principle of the last line with a 3-6-3-4 syllabic pattern signalling the poem's close.

15 The blue bamboo hat and the green straw raincoat refer to nature and symbolise the hermit's humble life.

16 This line is a quotation from an old story in which the fisherman advised Qu Yuan (Gul Won in Korean), who was devastated about his banishment from the court, not to be affected by circumstances.

17 This line mentions the story of Wu Zixu (O Ja-seo in Korean) who was outraged at the betrayal of his king.

18 The loyal subject is Qu Yuan who did not listen to the fisherman's advice and eventually committed suicide. In this stanza we can see the poet's conflicting thoughts. On the one hand, he wishes to free himself from attachment, but on the other he cannot help but remain concerned about the world's problems.

19 The blue bottle fly's commonly known attraction to excrement here symbolises the courtier's propensity to engage in flattery.

20 Sang the Courtier was a famous man who was primarily concerned

with finance. If the speaker were to be overheard by him, the courtier would advise him to take advantage of his skills in finance in order to flatter the king.

21 When looking at the shadow on the moon, Asian people identified this image.

22 This reference is to the legend about an old Chinese man who washed his ears out when the emperor proposed his name as an heir to his throne. He did so because he thought that even hearing about gaining power threatened his purity.

23 'A white cloud' symbolises his political enemies.

24 Xiaoxiang (Sosang in Korean) River and Dongting (Dongjeong in Korean) Lake in China are famous for their beautiful scenery. They evoked lyrical emotions for Joseon literati.

25 The term 'harsh winds' symbolises his political enemies.

26 This is from a Chinese story involving a general who beat a pond of ducks in order to make sufficient noise to deceive his enemy into believing that his army was bigger than it actually was. The attempt was successful. The reference to 'shame' indicates the Manchu War of 1636 which forced the poet into hiding.

27 The line 'our way of life in Cangzhou' (Changju in Korean) refers to the attitude to life of the fisherman who gave advice to Qu Yuan (Gul Won in Korean) not to dwell on worldly concerns and to live one's life freely and naturally. Cangzhou is the name of the lake from 'Song of the fisherman'.

28 Qili (Chilli in Korean) River refers to a famous hermit whose name is Yan Ziling (Um Ja-reung in Korean).

29 After ten years, Lyu shang (Yeo Sang in Korean) eventually met the ideal king and they made the Zhou Dynasty (1046–256 BC),

which was to become a great empire.

30 The 'pine tree window' refers to the translucent paper that serves as a window with the silhouette of the pine tree appearing on it. A pine tree is a symbol of loyalty. At the end of this long poem the poet remains resolute in his allegiance to the king.

31 Gyemyon-jo is one of the melodies in traditional Korean music. It emits a soft, melancholy sound.

32 Geomungo is the name of a traditional Korean musical instrument with six strings. In the past, the Yangban (upper class men) who understood and held a deep appreciation for music enjoyed playing the geomungo as part of their self-development.

33 Jungyang falls on 9 September. In Yin-Yang theory, the number nine symbolises extreme Yang. The date of double Yang is 9 September. On this day, people hike up a mountain and drink chrysanthemum wine to celebrate what is considered to be an auspicious day.

34 Ondol is the traditional Korean heating system which lies beneath the flagstone floor and heats it. The literal meaning of ondol is hot stone.

35 'Jade green brook' indicates a member of the royal family named Byuk Gye-su (碧溪守), which is homonymous with 'Jade green brook'. His original name was Lee Jong-suk (1508-?). Hwang Jin-i was known by the sobriquet 'Bright Moon'. This song was composed in order to seduce him.

36 The Jeopdong bird has a long history as a popular trope in Korean literature as well as in modern poetry and originated in a legend about a Chinese emperor who was dethroned. This bird, which has a beak that is red on the inside as well as the outside, is believed to cry until it spews blood when it feels resentment.

In this sijo, the bird's resentment stems from losing its lover.

37 'South of the river' is the place where seasonal birds migrate before the onset of winter. The wild goose was regarded as a messenger between separated people.

강호사시가 맹사성, 1360-1438

맹사성은 고려 왕조의 관료였으나 태조(재위. 1392-1398)가 조선을 건국한 뒤, 태조에서 세종(재위. 1418-1450)에 이르기까지 새 왕조의 군주들을 모셨다. 세종대에는 좌의정에 올랐을 정도로 성공적인 정치생활을 하였으며 76세에 관직에서 물러났다. 사계절의 순환을 찬양하는 주제를 지닌 다른 시조들과 마찬가지로, 이 시조에서 맹사성은 관직에서 물러나 그가 항상 바라던 삶을 영위할 수 있도록 훌륭한 정치를 베풀어준 임금의 은혜를 칭송하였다.

Song of the four seasons at the lake world Maeng Sa-seong, 1360-1438

Maeng Sa-seong was a court bureaucrat during the Goryeo Dynasty. However, when King Taejo (r. 1392-1398) established Joseon, he devoted himself to serving the new kings from Taejo to Sejong (r. 1418-1450). He led a successful career as the Left State Councillor during King Sejong's reign and retired from his duty when he was seventy-six. In common with other sijo on this theme of the four seasons' blessing, he gave credit to the king's benevolence for granting him the kind of retirement that he had always desired.

어부단가 이현보, 1467-1555

이현보는 연산군(재위. 1494-1506)과 중종(재위. 1506-1544) 시절의 관료였다. 그는 정치적 혼란 속에서 관료생활을 했기 때문에 44년 동안 관직에 있으면서 내내 정적으로부터 끊임없는 위협을 받아야 했다. 마침내 관직에서 물러나 고향인 경상도 안동으로 돌아온 후, 작가가 알려져 있지 않은 어부 노래들을 기반으로 이 시조를 창작하였다.

Short songs of a fisherman Lee Hyun-bo, 1467-1555

Lee Hyun-bo was a court bureaucrat during the reign of the disgraced King Yeonsan (1494-1506) as well as that of King Jungjong (1506-1544). He served forty-four years amidst a background of political turmoil. Therefore, his entire career was marked by continual threats from his political enemies. When he finally retired and returned to his home town (Andong, Gyeongsang province), he wrote this sijo based on the many anonymously written songs about a fisherman.

도산십이곡 이황, 1501-1570

이황은 중종(재위. 1506-1544), 명종(재위. 1545-1567), 선조(재위. 1567-1608) 시절의 관료였다. 그는 일생 동안 위대한 성리학자로 평가 받았으며, 오늘날에도 그 명성이 이어지고 있다. 많은 왕들이 그를 등용하고자 하였으나 그는 관직을 괴롭게 여기며 학문에 몰두하고자 힘썼다. 무려 53번이나 사직 의사를 밝혔지만 그를 붙잡아 두려는 왕들의 고집에 의해 번번이 무산되었다.

이 작품은 이황이 잠시 관직에서 벗어나 경상도 안동에 위치한 도산서원에 머무를 때 창작되었다. 도산서원은 이황으로 인해 유교문화의 핵심장소로 알려져 있다. 이 시조에서 이황은 학문에 대한 열망과 이를 가능케 하는 은자로서의 삶에 대한 갈망을 표현하였다.

Twelve songs at Dosan Lee Hwang, 1501-1570

Lee Hwang was a court bureaucrat during the reigns of Jungjong (1506-1544), Myeongjong (1545-1567), and Seonjo (1567-1608). He was regarded as a great Neo-Confucian scholar during his lifetime, as he still is in the present day. Many kings summoned him to serve at the court but he resisted this because he wanted to devote himself to his studies. He tried to resign as many as fifty-three times but he could not do so due to the insistence of the various kings that he served.

This song was written just after he had temporarily retired to Dosan Seowon (Neo-Confucian academy) in Andong, Gyeongsang province, which is known as the centre of Neo-Confucian culture largely due to Lee Hwang's legacy. Here he expresses his devotion to study and longing for the life of the hermit which makes it possible.

정철 시조 정철, 1536-1593

정철은 명종(재위. 1545-1567), 선조(재위. 1567-1608) 시절의 관료였다. 그는 아버지와 큰형이 정쟁에 패하여 조정에서 추방당하게 된 사건으로 힘든 어린 시절을 보내야 했다. 한양(현재의 서울)에서 태어났음에도, 정철은 10대 후반 호남지역(현재의 전라도)에 정착하기 전까지 이곳저곳을 떠돌아다녀야 했다. 그러나 호남에서 정철은 스승과 벗들을 만나 오늘날 호남 가단으로 잘 알려진 문단을 형성하였다. 그들의 문학적 능력은 가사라고 불리는 또 다른 국문 시가 장르를 창작할 때 꽃을 피웠으며, 정철도 전 시대에 걸쳐 가장 위대한 가사 작가로 평가받다. 그러나 시조 시행의 길이를 파격적으로 늘린 사설시조를 창작하고, 술과 같은 범속한 주제들을 도입했다는 면에서, 그가 시조 장르에 기여한 바 또한 주목할 만한 가치가 있다.

Sijo written by Jeong Cheol Jeong Cheol, 1536-1593

Jeong Cheol was a court bureaucrat during the reigns of King Myeongjong (1545-1567) and King Seonjo (1567-1608). He went through a particularly tough childhood due to the banishment of his father and eldest brother from the court as a result of their involvement on the losing side of a political debate. Although he was born in Hanyang (today's Seoul), he had to wander around until he settled down in the Honam area (today's Jeolla province) in his late teens. However, in Honam he met his teacher and true friends. They formed a literary group, which is known as Honam Gadan (song group) today, and wrote numerous songs in Korean. Their literary gift blossomed when they wrote the alternative Korean song genre known as Gasa. Indeed, Jeong Cheol has been called the greatest Gasa poet of all time. Although he is best known for this work, his contributions to sijo are also worthy of attention, including his innovative extension of the number of lines and his introduction of lowbrow themes including references to alcohol.

방옹시여 신흠, 1566-1628

신흠은 선조(재위. 1567-1608) 시절의 관료였다. 그는 조선 중기의 가장 위대한 네 명의 한문학 작가 중 한 명으로 평가된다. 선조는 신흠을 포함한 7명의 신하들을 선발하여 자신이 죽은 후 남겨질 어린 세자를 돌봐 줄 것을 부탁하였다. 이후 광해군(재위. 1608-1623)이 어린왕의 어린 세자를 제치고 왕좌를 차지했을 때, 7명의 신하들은 목숨을 위협받았다. 신흠 또한 조정에서 추방당하였고 끊임없는 처벌 위협을 느끼며 살아야 했다. 이 시기 동안 그는 '방옹시여'라고 불리는 30수의 시조를 창작하였다.

Songs by an exiled old man Shin Heum, 1566-1628

Shin Heum was a court bureaucrat during King Seonjo's reign (1567-1608). He is regarded as one of the four great writers of Sino-Korean literature of the mid-Joseon Dynasty. King Seonjo selected seven courtiers, including Shin Heum, and asked them to look after his young son upon his death. When the disgraced King Gwanghae (r. 1608-1623) took the throne after defeating the king's young son, the seven courtiers were threatened with death. Shin Heum was banished from the court and lived under constant threat of further royal punishment. During this time, he wrote thirty sijo called 'Songs by an exiled old man'.

어부사시사 윤선도, 1587-1671

윤선도는 한국 문학사에서 가장 뛰어난 시조 작가이다. 그는 부유한 집안에서 출생하여 지방 관료로서 관직생활을 시작하였다. 30세 되던 때 광해군(재위. 1608-1623) 치하에서 막강한 권력을 휘두른 신하를 탄핵하고자 시도하였으나 실패하였고, 그 결과로 함경도의 먼 북방 지역으로 추방당했다. 윤선도는 완고한 성격으로 정적들과 결코 타협하지 않았고, 몇 차례 조정에 복귀했다가 다시 추방당하는 일을 겪었다.

1636년 병자호란 당시, 윤선도는 반정으로 광해군을 몰아내고 왕이 된 인조(재위. 1623-1649)를 구하기 위해 배를 타고 한양으로 오는 길에 인조가 결국 청나라 왕에게 항복한 소식을 듣게 되었다. 윤선도는 그 길로 배를 돌려 제주도에 들어가 은신하고자 하였으나, 제주도로 향하는 길에 아름다운 경치를 지닌 보길도라는 섬을 지나며 그곳에 은거하기로 결정하였다. 이 작품은 그가 스스로 조정을 등진 10년의 세월 동안 지은 것이다.

Song of a fisherman's four seasons Yun Seon-do, 1587–1671

Yun Seon-do is the most renowned sijo poet in Korean history. He was born into a rich family and started his career as a local official. At the age of thirty he attempted but failed to impeach the most powerful courtier during the disgraced King Gwanghae's reign (1608–1623) with the end result that Yun Seon-do was banished to the far north area of Hamgyung province. Yun Seon-do's notorious stubbornness left him unable to reconcile with his political enemies and he returned to and was banished from the court several more times.

During the Manchu War of 1636, Yun Seon-do sailed to King Injo (r. 1623–1649) who had succeeded the King Gwanghae in a rebellion in an effort to save the king, but on his way he heard the news that the king had surrendered to the Manchu king. He turned back his boat immediately and tried to hide himself on Jeju Island. On his way to Jeju he came across Bogil Island, which has beautiful scenery, and decided to hide there. This song was written during his ten-year self-imposed exile from the political world.

전원사시가 신계영, 1577–1669

신계영은 광해군(재위. 1608–1623), 인조(재위. 1623–1649), 효종(재위. 1649–1659) 시절의 관료였다. 이 책에 소개한 다른 관료들과는 달리, 신계영은 관직생활을 시작하기 전 17년 동안 고향 예산(충청도)에 머물렀다. 관직생활을 하면서도 종종 예산으로 돌아왔고 마침내 79세 때 관직에서 물러났다. 17세기의 시조 작가들은 성리학의 철학적 사고보다는 일상 생활을 작품에 담는 경향을 보인다. 오랜 기간 고향 지방에 머물렀던 생활 덕분에, 신계영의 시조는 이러한 시조의 새 흐름을 대표하게 되었다.

Pastoral songs of the four seasons Shin Gye-young, 1577–1669

Shin Gye-young was a court bureaucrat during the reigns of Gwanghae (the disgraced king who reigned from 1608 to 1623), Injo (1623–1649), and Hyojong (1649–1659). Unlike the other bureaucrats in this book, he stayed in his local province (Yesan, Chungcheong) for seventeen years before serving as an official. During his period of duty, he repeatedly returned to Yesan and finally retired from his duty when he was seventy-nine. During the seventeenth century, sijo poets tended to reflect upon their daily life in their sijo rather than Neo-Confucian philosophical thought. Due to his lengthy life in his local province, Shin's sijo exemplifies this new current within sijo.

전가팔곡 이휘일, 1619-1672

이휘일은 경상도 지역의 문인으로서 관직생활을 하지 않았다. 그는 위대한 성리학자, 이황의 학문적 유산을 이어받았다. 이 시조는 땅을 경작하는 노동에 대한 실제적인 묘사로 시조 연구자들 사이에서 주목 받았다. 그러나 문인이었던 이휘일은 직접 농사에 참여하지는 않았다. 대신, 자기 고장의 농부들이 열심히 일할 수 있도록 장려하였으며 자연과의 조화를 이루는 삶을 살았다.

Eight pastoral songs Lee Hwi-il, 1619-1672

Lee Hwi-il was a member of the literati in Gyeongsang province who did not serve at the court. He inherited the legacy of the greatest Neo-Confucian scholar, Lee Hwang. This sijo has been highlighted by sijo researchers due to its realistic depiction of the labour that was involved in cultivating a field. However, as a scholar he did not personally work in the field. Instead, he encouraged the local common people to work hard and live in harmony with nature.

황진이 시조 황진이, 16세기

황진이는 기생이었다. 기생은 상층 남성들을 위해 친교와 유흥을 제공하는 여성들로서, 음악과 시에 재능을 가지고 있었다. 그들의 역할은 일본의 게이샤와 비견된다. 현재 우리가 알고 있는 황진이의 일생은 야담이라고 불리는 책들의 내용을 따른 것이다. 이 책들에 따르면 황진이는 많은 사대부들을 유혹했으며, 단지 허세만 가득한 학자들과 진짜 학자들을 구별해 내는 능력을 갖추고 있었다. 그러한 능력은 그녀가 시조에서 자신의 연정 대상인 남성들을 비판하는 모습에도 반영되어 있다. 황진이는 그들을 존경할 만한 자격이

없거나 열등한 대상처럼 취급하기도 하고, 그들의 열정에 무관심한 반응을
표현하기도 하였다.

Sijo written by Hwang Jin-i Hwang Jin-i, 16c

Hwang Jin-i worked as a kisaeng. Kisaeng were women who provided
company and entertainment for men and possessed skills in music
and poetry. Their role bears comparison with Japanese geisha. Our
knowledge of her life is confined to the details given in the story
books named Ya Dam, which literally means non-orthodox stories.
Hwang Jin-i was included in them because she seduced a number
of Neo-Confucian literati and possessed the ability to identify
genuine scholars from mere pseudo-scholars. Such perception is
also reflected in her willingness to criticise her lovers in her sijo, even
viewing them as inferior and unworthy of respect and expressing
feelings of indifference toward their passion for her.

김천택 시조 김천택, 18세기

김천택은 양반과 평민 사이에 위치한 중인 계층에 속한 인물로, 포교이자 유
명한 시조 가객이었다. 중인 계층인 그는 자신이 속한 신분의 제약을 잘 알고
있었다. 김천택은 1728년에 가객으로서의 전문성을 발휘하여 『청구영언』
이라는 시조집을 역사상 처음으로 편찬하였다. 그전까지 시조는 가창자들
에 의해 구전되어 왔었다. 김천택은 많은 시조들이 시간이 지남에 따라 잊혀
지게 될 것을 우려하여 시조집을 편찬한 것이다. 시조 작품들을 보존하려는
그의 노력 덕분에 현대인들도 시조를 감상할 수 있게 되었다.

Sijo written by Kim Cheon-taek Kim Cheon-taek, 18c

Kim Cheon-taek, a renowned sijo singer, was said to have been a
sheriff, which means he belonged to a middle class between the
Yangban (upper class) and Pyeongmin (common people). He was
keenly aware of the restrictions which this status placed upon him.
He drew on his performance background in order to edit the first sijo
anthology, which is called *Cheonggu Youngun* (*The Everlasting Songs
of Joseon*), in 1728. Before then, sijo was transmitted orally by singers.

He was concerned that a great many sijo songs had been forgotten with the passing of time. Due to his contribution to the preservation of sijo songs, Koreans are able to read sijo in modern times.

박효관 시조 박효관, 19세기

박효관은 19세기의 유명한 시조 가객이다. 김천택과 마찬가지로 중인 계층에 속했으나, 박효관의 후원자는 고종(재위. 1863-1907)의 아버지로, 당시 막강한 권세를 자랑하던 대원군이었다. 박효관은 자신의 신분에 구애 받지 않고, 시조 작품을 짓고 연행하는 삶에 만족하였다. 그의 작품 대다수는 사랑에 관한 것인데, 이때의 사랑은 왕에 대한 충성심을 은유한 것이 아니라는 점에서 18세기부터 주류를 형성해 오던 기생들의 시조와 유사하다. 박효관 또한 1876년에 『가곡원류』라는 시조집을 편찬하였다.

Sijo written by Park Hyo-gwan Park Hyo-gwan, 19c

Park Hyo-gwan was a famous nineteenth-century sijo singer. Like Kim Cheon-taek, he belonged to the middle class, however, he had no additional position and his patron was the powerful father of King Gojong (r. 1863-1907) the Daewongun (the regent). Unlike Kim Cheon-taek, he was not concerned by his class. He was able to derive satisfaction from writing and performing his work. The majority of his poems are about love, however, not as a conventional metaphor for loyalty to the king. This represents a striking similarity to the sijo of the Kisaeng, which had become mainstream from the eighteenth century onwards. He also edited a sijo anthology entitled *Gakok Wolryu* (*The Original Stream of Sijo Songs*) in 1876.

K-포엣 스페셜 에디션

시조,
서정시로 새기다

2019년 6월 10일 초판 1쇄 발행

지은이 맹사성, 이현보, 이황, 정철, 신흠, 윤선도, 신계영, 이휘일, 황진이, 김천택, 박효관
편역 고정희, 저스틴 M. 바이런-데이비스 | 펴낸이 김재범
편집장 김형욱 | 편집 강민영 | 관리 강초민, 홍희표 | 디자인 나루기획
인쇄·제책 굿에그커뮤니케이션 | 종이 한솔PNS
펴낸곳 (주)아시아 | 출판등록 2006년 1월 27일 제406-2006-000004호
주소 경기도 파주시 회동길 445(서울 사무소: 서울특별시 동작구 서달로 161-1 3층)
전화 02.821.5055 | 팩스 02.821.5057 | 홈페이지 www.bookasia.org
ISBN 979-11-5662-317-5 (set) | 979-11-5662-410-3 (04810)
값은 뒤표지에 있습니다.

K-Poet Special Edition

Encounters with the Korean Lyrical Spirit
An Anthology of Sijo

Written by Maeng Sa-seong, Lee Hyun-bo, Lee Hwang, Jeong Cheol, Shin Heum,
Yun Seon-do, Shin Gye-young, Lee Hwi-il, Hwang Jin-i, Kim Cheon-taek, Park Hyo-gwan
Selected and translated by Ko Jeong-hee and Justin M. Byron-Davies
Address 445, Hoedong-gil, Paju-si, Gyeonggi-do, Korea
(Seoul Office:161-1, Seodal-ro, Dongjak-gu, Seoul, Korea)
Homepage Address www.bookasia.org | **Tel** (822).821.5055 | **Fax** (822).821.5057
ISBN 979-11-5662-317-5 (set) | 979-11-5662-410-3 (04810)
First published in Korea by ASIA Publishers 2019